The Village

Alton Gansky

Bill Myers and Angela Hunt

AMARIS MEDIA
INTERNATIONAL

Published by Amaris Media International.
Copyright © 2016 Alton Gansky
Cover Design: Angela Hunt
Photo © lctrail @ fotolia.com

ISBN-13: 978-0692669143
ISBN-10: 0692669140

www.harbingersseries.com

HARBINGERS

A novella series by

Bill Myers, Angela Hunt, and Alton Gansky

In this fast-paced world with all its demands, the four of us wanted to try something new. Instead of the longer novel format, we wanted to write something equally as engaging but that could be read in one or two sittings—on the plane, waiting to pick up the kids from soccer, or as an evening's read.

We also wanted to play. As friends and seasoned novelists, we thought it would be fun to create a game we could participate in together. The rules were simple:

Rule 1
Each of us would write as if we were one of the characters in the series:
- Bill Myers would write as Brenda, the street-hustling tattoo artist who sees images of the future.
- Frank Peretti will write as the professor, the atheist ex-priest ruled by logic.

3

- Angela Hunt would write as Andi, the professor's brilliant-but-geeky assistant who sees inexplicable patterns.

• Alton Gansky would write as Tank, the naïve, big-hearted jock with a surprising connection to a healing power.

Rule 2

Instead of the four of us writing one novella together (we're friends but not crazy), we would write it like a TV series. There would be an overarching story line into which we'd plug our individual novellas, with each story written from our character's point of view.

We started with *The Call, The Haunted, The Sentinels,* and *The Girl.* Round two brought us *The Revealing, Infestation, Infiltration,* and *The Fog.* Round three? *Leviathan, The Mind Pirates, Hybrids,* and now, *The Village.* And if we keep having fun, we'll begin a fourth round and so on until other demands pull us away or, as in TV, we get cancelled.

There you have it. We hope you'll find these as entertaining in the reading as we did in the writing.

Bill, Angie, and Al

barbs. Just as well. She hasn't been all that warm and cuddly since—

Well, no need to get into that now.

Seated behind me was Daniel, my ten-year-old buddy. He wasn't himself. I expected to see his young face hovering over the screen of his handheld video game like usual. I hadn't heard a single digital beep out of that game—or a word out of him.

Of course, I had no right to expect anything to be normal.

My friends and I have been living in a "new normal." That's what Andi called it. She's good with words, and the Internet, and research, and patterns, and just about everything else. She is really good at keeping me on pins and needles. Anyway, she's especially good at seeing patterns no one else can see. She can look at ten unrelated things and see what connects them all. That's our Andi. Now that the professor is gone, Andi Goldstein is the smart one of our group. If I said that out loud I'm sure she'd show me the back of her hand. Brenda might show me the front of her fist.

That's not to say that Brenda Barnick is any kind of dummy. She's smart in a different kinda way. *Street smart* is the best way to describe her. She's a gifted artist, although most of her art decorates people's skin. No one can ink a tat like Brenda. She's dynamite with pen and paper too. The strange thing—not so strange to us these days—is that her drawings somehow show a bit of the future.

Me? Well, if we haven't already met, then all you need to know is that my name is Bjorn Christensen but I go by Tank. It's easier to say. At six-foot-three and 260 pounds, I've been gaining weight, so no one

Chapter 1

ARRIVAL

THE SUN WAS blinking. Well, not really blinking. That would be a sign that the end of the world was about to arrive. What it was doing was flashing in my eyes as I did my best to drive the Ford SUV up the narrow mountain road. The real culprits were the trees. It was about an hour from sunset and dogwood trees kept blocking the sun, making it look like it was flickering. Truth be told, it was kinda annoying. Still the forest, the mountains, the clear sky was all very beautiful and very different from the place we left that morning.

I wished it were that lovely inside the car.

I shot a glance at Andi sitting in the passenger seat next to me, then stole a quick look at the backseat. Brenda sat behind Andi gazing out the window on her right just as she had been doing since we left the airport in Asheville. She hadn't said more than twenty words since we arrived in North Carolina from our stay at Andi's grandparents' home near Tampa. If you knew Brenda, then you know how this was not normal for her. Not a single snide remark. Odd, I found myself missing her occasional asks, "So, why do they call you Tank?" My size is why Daniel sat behind me while I drove. He didn't need as much leg room as Andi and Brenda.

"Much farther?"

Whoo-hoo. Two words from Brenda.

Andi kept her eyes on her smartphone. "GPS says about five minutes, but it's been on-again-off-again. Cell coverage up here is abysmal."

Double whoo-hoo. This was almost a conversation. I decided to risk it and say something myself. "The road is slowing us down. Too narrow. Too many hairpin curves."

"Ya think?" Brenda sounded sour. "I'm getting carsick." There was a pause and I redirected the rearview mirror to get a better look at her face. She was staring at me. "And when I get carsick, Cowboy, I tend to vomit forward and to the left. Just about where you're sitting."

Brenda liked to call me "Cowboy." No one else does. "Should I stop and give you a chance to . . . you know . . . let you get some air."

The three in the car all said, "No!" Even little Daniel.

"Okay, okay. Cool your jets. I'm just trying to keep everyone safe."

"I'm sick of the car," Brenda said. "I'm sick of flying to out of the way places."

"Technically," I said, "Tampa is not out of the way. It's a pretty big city. And when we were in San Diego—"

"Shut up, Bjorn."

Yikes. Brenda never uses my first name.

"Yes, ma'am. Shutting up."

Andi's guess of five minutes was a tad off. Not by much, just a quarter hour. Brenda would have chewed through the car door if she could have managed it, and a big part of me believed she could.

By the time we rolled into town, the sun had dipped below the mountains and what had once been shadows was now full blown twilight. The streetlights, which looked a hundred years old if they were a day, flickered on and made a brave effort at pushing back the dark of evening. I was glad to pull onto Main Street and leave the twisty two-lane road behind. Newland, North Carolina wasn't all that far from Asheville, but it was all up hill.

"No cell service, guys," Andi said. "We'll have to find the hotel the old fashioned way. Look for it."

"You made reservations, right?" Brenda made the question sound like a statement.

Andi shook her head. Her flighty red hair flopped around a little. Some might think it looked funny, but I think she's adorable. As far as I'm concerned, she is gorgeous from the tiptop of her hair down to those tiny things she calls feet.

"I couldn't make reservations. They don't have a website and when I called all I got was an answering service. And by answering service I mean answering machine. Didn't know those things were still around."

Brenda leaned forward and for a moment I thought there would be three people in the front seat. "You're kidding me, right?"

"C'mon, Brenda. I'm not known for my sense of humor."

That wasn't completely true. I'd seen Andi laugh many times. She could be witty when she wanted. I'm pretty sure she wasn't feeling it at the moment.

"I'm not spending the night in the car." Brenda said that with some heat.

"We shouldn't have to." Andi didn't bother to turn to face Brenda. "You know how this works. We get a message with a destination and information on where to stay. Maybe our keepers made reservations for us."

"They had better."

"Okay, ladies," I said, "let's see what we're dealing with before we start shooting at each other." Of course, for self-protection, I glanced over my shoulder to see if Brenda was coming for me. She wasn't. Instead, I saw little Daniel patting her leg. Daniel might be the only person in the world who can settle Hurricane Brenda. It was working.

I motored slowly down the street, taking in the town. There wasn't much to take in. I've been in a few small towns in my time and this one was pretty much the same thing. The buildings were old, maybe built in the 30s and 40s. Some were made of red brick, some had wood exteriors. I didn't see any stucco like what I see in California. There were a few shops and one department store, though most would be hard pressed to call the small two-story building much of a department store. There were two eating establishments that I hoped offered biscuits and gravy, and a bar for those that liked to drink their meals from a beer mug. I slowed when I came to a building with a gold star on the door and a sign that read *Sheriff's Office*.

I pulled to the curb. A sign hung on the door: GONE FISHING. We saw a hardware store, a feed store, a shoe store, and a few other stores.

"Anyone else notice the weirdness?" Andi was leaning forward as if by doing so, the town would release its secrets.

"Like what?" Brenda asked.

"Like there's no one on the street. No pedestrians. No cars on the road. I don't even see parked cars. Shouldn't there be a beat up pickup truck or something?"

"Maybe . . ." I began.

"Maybe what?" Andi said.

I put my brain in high gear, then said, "I got nuthin'."

"Tank's got nothing." Daniel snickered. At least the kid hadn't forgotten how to talk. He was a quiet kid most of the time. *Emotionally challenged* his doctors say, but he's not. He's just different, and since Brenda took over his care, he is more open than ever. Not a chatterbox, but he no longer hesitates to speak. He has a special gift all his own.

"Hey! I thought you were my pal." I said the words with a big grin.

"I am. Pals. You still got nuthin'."

I caught Brenda and Andi smiling. Sometimes I think the kid could walk into a dark room with no lights and somehow lights would come on anyway. Don't analyze the statement. Just take it at face value.

We reached the end of Main Street and I saw something that gave me hope—a church. A church with a real steeple. It was small, but beautiful. I'm the spiritual one of the group and I love church. My friends, well they haven't come around. Yet.

10

Just as we reached the end of Main Street Andi piped up. "There. I see the hotel. On the left."

There was movement in the backseat as Daniel and Brenda scooted forward for a look-see.

"I see it." I did and it looked good to me. I was sick of the car. At first it was hard to make out detail in the dim light, but I could see clearly enough to know I was looking at a three-story, wood-framed building with an attractive front porch and shutters on the windows. The place looked very much like a country home on steroids. It wasn't actually in town, but about a hundred yards past the last building on the street. As we drew near, I could see someone had kept the place up. The paint looked new, the shutters hung straight, the furniture—about six or so rocking chairs—was very inviting, although, after a flight and a slow drive, I was looking forward to standing for a bit.

"Looks nice," Andi said. "I like the exterior."

Brenda huffed. "I'm more interested in the interior. I really gotta pee."

With that pressing news, I pulled into the parking lot on the east side of the building, took the first space I could find—which was easy since ours was the only car in the lot—and switched off the SUV.

Brenda's door was open before I could set the parking brake.

GETTING A COLD SHOULDER

"I'M GONNA WAIT to get the luggage," I said. "I want to make sure we're staying here tonight."

"It has to be here," Andi said. "This is where we were sent and it's the only place in town, at least as far as I saw."

I agreed with that. I hadn't seen anything that said "motel" or "hotel" or boarding house and I mentioned that fact. "Come on, buddy." I put a hand on Daniel's small shoulder. "Let's go see if Brenda made it to the necessary room."

Daniel giggled. "Necessary room." He repeated the phrase then snickered again.

We walked to the front of the old style hotel, up four steps to the front porch and to a wide green door with stain glass panels. Light oozed through the colored glass making me think of the church again.

Andi pushed the door open. It wasn't fully closed. Apparently Brenda's need was real. The lobby looked like something out of the 1950s. The carpet was ornate and decorated with images of flowers. The flowers had faces. I think they were meant to be cute, but they kinda creeped me out. I shut the door behind us, then turned my attention to the front of the lobby. The front desk was made of wood that bore a shiny bar-top finish. It was as pretty as the carpet was disturbing.

A small woman stood behind the front desk. She was short and—I hate to say this—looked like a mouse. I don't mean she had mouse ears, I mean her features were small, her nose slightly pointed, and her hair a light brown that looked like it wanted to be blond. For a moment, I started to look for mouse whiskers. Her eyes were wide, but that was easy to understand. A black woman with dreadlocks had just plunged through the lobby door and made a beeline for . . . I looked around the lobby . . . the bathroom next to the stairs. Brenda always made a strong first impression.

I felt a smile might do the lady some good, so I gave her my best we're-not-criminals grin and walked to the desk. "My name is Tank. This is Andi Goldstein, and this little guy is Daniel."

"Um, hello."

She even sounded a little like a mouse. I continued. "I'm guessing you already saw Brenda. She's about the same height as Andi and—"

"The black girl with the funny hair?" the woman said.

"That's her. We've been on the road for a long time and she needed . . . to use the facilities."

"I figured that part out."

Andi moved to my side. "I called and left a message yesterday on your machine but never got a call back."

I heard a flushing sound followed by a door opening. Brenda exited, looking refreshed. "Sorry about that, but when a girl has got to go, a girl has got to go."

Andi returned to the desk clerk. "Anyway, we would like three rooms, please."

"I-I'm sorry. We're full up."

We stood dumbfounded. I started to say something, but Andi had taken control. "If you were booked-up, then why didn't you return my call and tell us that before we drove up here."

"I didn't get the message. Maybe someone else did." The woman inched back a foot as if she expected Andi to spring over the counter.

I watched as Andi's eyes shifted to a name plate on the counter. "Jewel Tarkington. That's a lovely name. Listen, Ms. Tarkington. I think you're having some fun with us. Maybe Brenda's mad dash in here put you off a little, but we're really nice people and need a place to stay tonight."

"I wish I could help."

"Our money is good," I added.

"I have no doubt that you are wonderful people, but like I say, the hotel is—"

"There are no cars in the parking lot," Brenda said. The temperature in the room dropped at least five degrees.

"We don't use cars much around here—"

"I see you keep your keys on that board behind you," Andi said. "It looks to me like every hook has a key hanging from it. Did everyone leave at the same time?"

"No, of course not, it's just that . . . that . . ."

Daniel spoke to Brenda softly but I heard him just fine. "Like Tank. She's got nuthin'."

14

I half expected Brenda to hush my little buddy but she didn't. I don't think I would have either.

"Let me see if I have this right, lady. No cars in the lot, no one in their rooms, no noise from people staying here, and you want us to believe that every room in the place is booked. You expecting a bus or somethin'?"

"Please, there's nothing I can do." Jewel began to look a little pale. "I can call another hotel for you. You know. Get you booked there."

"This town has another hotel?" I asked.

"Well, no. I didn't mean in Newland, I meant somewhere else. There's a hotel up the road a piece. I hear it's real nice."

"How far up the road?" Andi's words were coming out a little sharper than usual.

"Not far. Just fifty or sixty miles."

"Fifty or sixty miles!"

I could tell Brenda was about to launch herself over the counter. I put a hand on her shoulder and gave a little squeeze. She pressed her lips together so tight that I expected to hear one of them blow out like an old tire. A second later, Daniel was standing at her side. When I say standing at her side, I mean he had pressed himself against her leg. She put a hand on his shoulder kinda like I had put one of my mitts on her.

She took a ragged breath. "You're going to turn us out onto the street. You're telling us that the only thing we can do is take my son up a winding, narrow mountain road in the dark to some other hotel just so you don't have to bother with us?"

Daniel sniffed. I glanced at the boy. His lower lip quivered. His eyes were wet. He looked at the floor, then leaned his head against Brenda's hip as if sorrow had made it too heavy to hold erect. If I were a member of the group that nominates actors for the Oscars, I would put Daniel's name in for an award.

"Son?" Jewel looked from Daniel's white face to Brenda's ebony skin.

"What? You don't think a black woman can adopt a white kid? Is that what all this is about? Race?"

"No, of course not."

"Then what is the problem, lady?" Brenda's tone grew hotter. "You gonna throw us back into the dark rather than release three of your precious rooms?"

She looked out the front window. "I can't get you to leave, can I?"

"No ma'am." I smiled when I said that.

Jewel marched around the front desk, then beat feet to the front door. I watched and then waited for her to tell us to get out. Instead, she locked the door, twisting the deadbolt latch several times to make certain it had engaged. She then checked to make sure the front windows were still battened down. With brisk movements she closed the curtains over the window, taking a peek out as if expecting a visit from the local pitchfork-and-torch mob.

"Okay, okay. I'll give you three rooms." She hustled back behind the desk. "Do you mind walking up stairs? Our elevator doesn't work. Never had the money to get the thing fixed."

"Maybe that's because you keep sending paying customers away."

I wish Brenda hadn't said that. Jewel ignored her.

"We don't mind stairs," Andi said. I started to differ, but settled on being glad that I wouldn't be driving any more tonight.

"Thank you, ma'am." I gave my best smile again; the one I save for special occasions. "It'll only take me a moment to get the luggage from the car."

"No!" the mouse roared. "I mean, leave it. Get it in the morning."

"We have toiletries and clothes in there—"

"I don't care. I've already locked up." She looked at the door. "I don't see any more strangers walking in. If I had known you were coming I would have locked it before you got here."

"Why?" Brenda asked. "Does the boogie man live in Newland?"

"No. He left when he got scared." Jewel fidgeted with the keys. "Look, I'll let you stay for free. Just don't unlock the door. Got it?"

"No, I don't got it." Brenda's flame was growing hotter.

"This is the deal. You stay for free but you don't go out until the sun is up tomorrow. If you're hungry—"

"We are," I said.

She studied me with worried eyes for a moment. "A man your size must be hungry all the time."

"Not all the time . . . okay, you're right."

Jewel pointed to a door in the back wall and near the western corner. "That's the kitchen. Feel free to make a meal for yourself. There's eggs, bacon and the like. You can have breakfast for dinner." She paused to let another thought in. "There's some leftover fried chicken I made yesterday. Mashed potatoes and gravy, too. You'll have to heat that up, but it should fill the hole."

Fried chicken, potatoes, and gravy. I considered kissing Jewel on her little mouse nose.

"That's very kind of you."

I don't think she heard the compliment. "Stay away from the windows. And by all that is holy, don't open them."

"Until sunup, right?" Andi said. She gave me a knowing look that said *This woman is a couple of sandwiches shy of a picnic.*

"Right."

Andi pressed a little harder. "I don't suppose you want to explain all this. What are you afraid of?"

"You're right, ma'am, I don't want to explain it."

"Leave the woman alone," Brenda said. "We have rooms. Let's be happy about that."

Andi's expression said she wasn't satisfied with the suggestion, but she didn't object. When Brenda was right, Brenda was right.

"Good." Jewel pushed the keys forward. "Third floor. The windows look out the back and onto the mountains. Real pretty in the morning. The rooms don't have bathrooms. Halfway down the hall you'll find a men's and women's facility. Showers are in there, too. It takes a few minutes for the hot water to make its way up to the third floor, so be patient."

She reached beneath the counter and pulled out a handful of toothbrushes, still in their factory wrapping, thank the Lord, four combs, and four tiny hair brushes. She also retrieved those small bottles of shampoo, conditioner, and soap in a box. She was well stocked for all the people who didn't stay in her hotel.

18

We each said thank you, some of us more sincerely than others, and started up the stairs. I led the way. From behind me I heard Brenda say, "Nope, that wasn't weird at all." Yep, she is still the queen of sarcasm.

BREAKFAST FOR DINNER

THE ROOMS WERE nice enough. Not grand. Not even business class. Back in my college football playing days our football team had better rooms when we were out of town for away games. That was then; this was now. I guess most people would call the place quaint. The carpet was brown and looked clean; the bed looked like something dragged out of the fifties but with less style. There was an inexpensive dresser, a side chair, and an end table, all made from oak. The finish had yellowed over time. Still, there was nothing to complain about—except the wallpaper. Like the carpet in the lobby, the wallpaper reminded me of pictures I had seen of homes from the late 1800s. It was gaudy, overdone, and worse, had flowers with faces on them just like the lobby carpet. I didn't know if I could undress in front of all those tiny eyes. No wonder the hotel was empty. To anyone with an active imagination, this was a room designed to raise nightmares.

I also noticed that there was no phone in the room. I guess if you needed to contact the front desk you had to walk down three flights of stairs. In some ways the room was homey, if home was an empty old hotel run by a frightened, mousy woman.

Still, the place would do.

We didn't spend much time upstairs. I found the others standing in the hall just a few feet from my door.

"Did you see that wallpaper?" Andi asked. She looked a tad pale.

"Don't tell me," I said, "you want to get some for your place."

"Not a chance." Andi frowned. "Good thing I sleep with my eyes closed."

"I'm hungry." Daniel turned and marched to the stairs. The kid wasn't shy about such things.

"Since we have to go down to the first floor to eat," Brenda said, "I think we should slip out and get our luggage."

I reminded her that a promise was a promise and we had made a promise not to open the doors or windows. She called me a self-righteous side of beef. That was a new one. I didn't waste any brain cells trying to figure out if a side of beef could be righteous. I don't offend easily. "Small brain but thick hide," my father used to say. I suppose that's one reason he never won Father-of-the-Year.

Three flights of stairs later we were back in the lobby and moved into the kitchen. The kitchen, like the rest of the place, looked like a tribute to the finest appliances of the 50s. The good news was that Jewel had spoken the truth about the food. There was fried chicken and the makings for a decent breakfast. Since there wasn't enough chicken to go around, I offered to whip up some scrambled eggs,

21

bacon, and toast. Daniel liked the idea. Brenda and Andi insisted on helping.

We're normally a chatty bunch but there was little conversation while we worked. Brenda kept cutting her eyes to the window behind the heavy curtains.

"Our car is parked just outside that wall, right?" she asked.

"Yep."

"You know, I could slip out the window and—"

"C'mon, Brenda. Let it go." I turned the bacon over. It smelled heavenly. I was a little hungry when we started, now I was starved.

"She doesn't have the right to make demands like that. It's not like we're related to her. I ain't used to takin' orders from strangers. I ain't used to takin' orders from anybody."

This is where I miss the professor. He had a way of irritating Brenda into submission. He would say stuff like, "Use that brain of yours, Barnick." Of course, she would lash back but then she would tone down. The two drove each other bonkers and the rest of us had to go along for the ride.

But the professor wasn't here. Dr. James McKinney was a sixty something walking encyclopedia. In his younger days he had been a Jesuit priest, but something turned him sour on faith. He left the Jesuits, he left the Church, he left behind any belief he had in God and adopted a new Gospel—one that said there is no God and religion is a poison to society. The fact that I'm one of those evangelical Christians irritated him. It didn't matter. I wasn't going to change. Of course, I always hoped *he* would change. He did—some.

Then he killed himself.

Well, that's what the police said. He left a strange note which we still don't fully understand. Andi carries it with her all the time. She had been his assistant for years. Demanding as he was, he had become a father figure to her. I guess he became a father figure to all of us. We loved the cantankerous, irritable man with his constant I'm-smarter-than-you attitude. And he was right most of the time.

Brenda took his passing harder than she wanted us to know. She is a tough girl. When she gets her mad on she can frighten rabid dogs into fleeing. She was a force of nature and I did my best not to cross her. When we first learned the professor had gone missing we were frightened. Our missions have put us up against some very nasty people, but the professor's note sure made the suicide angle look true. Brenda showed little emotion at first, but we saw signs that the loss of the professor had gutted her like a fish. I caught her crying once and she threatened my life if I told anyone.

"What's eating you, Brenda?" Andi slipped eight fried eggs onto a platter we found in a cupboard. My suggestion of scrambled eggs got overruled. That's two a piece. I asked for only two eggs because I planned on eating a piece or two of the cold fried chicken in the fridge so I didn't want to overdo it.

"I didn't say anything was eatin' me."

I noticed she didn't make eye contact with Andi. No two women were more different than Andi and Brenda, and I don't mean the whole black and white thing. Andi was everything Brenda was not: easy going, brilliant, a whiz at research, and sociable; Brenda was everything Andi was not: forceful, opinionated, and a skilled artist. They were yin-and-

23

yang, tomato soup and grilled cheese. We were a better team when they were together than we were when one was missing.

Andi sighed. "Have it your way, girl. We're just your friends. You don't owe us anything."

That was harsh and I steeled myself waiting for Brenda to go ballistic. She didn't. And that scared the liver out of me. Instead she whispered one word: "Batman."

It doesn't take much to derail my train of thought, but that was so out of character and made so little sense I didn't know what to say. So I took the easy path. "Batman?"

I pulled the bacon out of the pan and set it on a paper towel covered platter. I studied Brenda as she buttered up some toast.

"Still hungry." Daniel said.

"Okay, buddy." I carried my load of fried pig strips to the table, Andi brought the platter of fried eggs, and Brenda delivered the toast. We sat and I said a silent prayer. The others have gotten used to me doing that and give me a minute or so of quiet at most meals. While I was at it, I prayed for wisdom. I had a feeling I was gonna need it.

We served ourselves, each ate a bite or two. Then Andi said, "Okay, girl, dish it. What's this about Batman?"

Brenda pushed her bacon around with her fork but didn't look up. That wasn't like her. Usually she looked you in the eye as if waiting for the right moment to spit in it.

She inhaled. I took a bite of toast. "You know about Batman, right?"

I shrugged. "Who doesn't? You are talking about the guy in the comic books, right?"

"Yes. I used to read them when I was a kid—when I could get them. What do you know about Batman?"

"You mean the character? Not the guys that created him," I said.

"Yeah, the character."

Andi looked at me.

"Batman is Bruce Wayne. When Wayne was a kid he saw his parents murdered in an alley of Gotham City. He dedicated his life to fighting crime. Studied. Trained. Became a famous superhero—although he's not really a superhero."

"He's not?" Daniel looked surprised.

I explained. "He doesn't have superpowers like Superman. He uses his training and skill to overcome bad guys."

"And?" Brenda prompted.

Clearly I had forgotten something. "Oh, and he had a sidekick named Robin."

"What do you know about Robin?"

I shrugged. Of course I read comics as a kid. Still read them occasionally, but I'm no expert. "He was called the 'Boy Wonder.' I think later he became the 'Teen Wonder.' If you want more detail, I'm going to disappoint you."

"I would do some research on the net," Andi said. "If I could get cell service up here."

"No need. I already did that." Brenda cut her egg but didn't eat any of it. She had something to say, but didn't want to say it. "I know Batman and Robin aren't real, but I've been thinking about them. Ever since I became Daniel's guardian. When I was a kid,

Batman and Robin were cool. When I became a parent, I began to see Batman as a lousy guardian. I know this is gonna sound crazy, but shouldn't someone have arrested Batman for child endangerment?"

That filled the room with silence, except for Daniel who wanted more bacon.

"I don't get it . . ." Then I got it. "You mean because Robin was a kid."

"Exactly, Tank. The adult Batman dragged the child Robin into situations where his life was in danger. They faced super-villains, hoods with guns and knives and all kinds of things meant to kill, and Batman saw no problem putting a minor in the middle of the fight. Today Bruce Wayne would be hauled off to court and Robin—Dick Grayson, I mean—would be put into foster care."

"Brenda," Andi said, "they're not real. That's all imagination and story telling."

Brenda looked at Daniel. "We're real."

I'm not always the brightest crayon in the box, but I got that connection.

Brenda pushed her plate to the side and Daniel swiped a slice of bacon off her plate. The kid had been hungry.

I did a quick search of all the closets in my brain looking for the right thing to say; the thing that would ease her mind. The closets were bare. I looked at Andi. Twice she looked ready to speak, but nothing emerged from her pretty mouth.

Brenda, however, still had things to say. "Think about what we've seen, what we've been through. We've seen things no one would believe. We've all been in danger and a few times we've come close to being takin' out. What happens to Daniel if. . .'"?

Since Daniel was sitting next to her, she didn't finish, but my brain, which was now running at top rpm, finished it for her: *What happens to Daniel if I'm killed while on one of these missions?* I was stunned by two things. First the question knocked me off my pins, then the fact that I had no answer finished me off.

Brenda kept at it. "This is . . . what? The *twelfth* time we've gone on some crazy mission. We've lived through horrible things. Dangerous things. Eyeless people, dead fish falling from the air, orbs that follow us around, ghostly things, mind stealing pirates—" she looked at me "—creatures that swim in fog and make meals outta people. Daniel was there. Tank, if you hadn't done what you did, we wouldn't be here now and I wouldn't be yammerin' like a crazy woman."

"You're not crazy, Brenda," I said. "And you're not yammering. We can tell this is important to you."

Boy, could I tell. Her eyes were wet and she kept biting her lip. A glance at Andi showed she suffered from the same wet eyes.

Brenda took a deep breath, but kept her eyes fixed on her plate of half-eaten food. "Now the professor's gone. As big a pain as he was in our corporate fannies, he was the real thinker among us. I don't mean no offense."

"None taken." Andi and I said that in unison.

"If it was too much for old man McKinney, then I can't figure out how we can do any better."

"He didn't kill himself," Andi said. "I told you I saw him in the mirror—"

"He's still gone, Andi." That was a whisper. Even upset as she was, Brenda couldn't bring herself to add to Andi's misery. We had grown pretty close since this roller coaster began.

"Where are you going with this?" Andi asked. "What's the punchline?"

Brenda leaned back in the chair, but didn't make eye-contact. I knew she was serious because Brenda had no problem staring into anyone's eyes, but at the moment she was softer than I had ever seen her.

"We quit," she said. "Me and Daniel. We're done. I can't be Batman and take a minor—" She looked at Daniel who had, for some reason, turned in his chair to stare at the curtains over the kitchen window; the one that looked out over the parking lot. "I shouldn't say 'minor.' I should say 'child.'"

After another ragged breath she continued. "I am Daniel's guardian. What kinda guardian am I when I drag him all over the place to face who-knows-what kind of dangers. Would you drag one of your loved ones into the situations we get into?"

That was a hard question to hear and an even harder one to answer. I couldn't think of anything to say. Andi, who always has something to say, remained silent.

If the conversation was upsetting to Daniel, then he didn't show it. He just kept staring at the drapes. Then he stood and moved toward the window.

I wanted to say, "Nothing is going to happen to Daniel. I'll see to that." It would have been a stupid thing to say. It was true, Daniel was with us, often helping us, during some pretty hairy situations that could have left us all dead. No one could promise safety to anyone else—

Daniel screamed.

Chapter 4

TOCKITY

I DON'T REMEMBER running to Daniel's side. I heard his tiny voice cry out and the next thing I knew I was next to him at the window. Outside the glass, his face no more than an inch from the pane, stood a man. An ugly man. A real mess of a man with wild hair, a beard that looked like it housed a family of rodents, and missing teeth. He was smiling in a way that kick-started my adrenaline.

I took Daniel by the back of his shirt and pulled him away from the window, turning him around. Brenda had him in her arms a second later. I kept my eyes glued to the face staring in at us. He had one blue eye; the other was covered with an eye-patch. The eye-patch was made from the top of a cereal box. The first three letters of *Corn*, as in *Corn Flakes*, were easy to read. His hair was a mass of brown and gray, and stuck out from his head in a hair-halo, or aura, or something. He wore a kind of overcoat. A *Mackintosh* I think they call it. I doubt it had been cleaned anytime in this decade. No wonder my little buddy let out a scream. At first I was tempted to do the same.

I stepped closer, but my size didn't seem to bother the guy any, he just stood there with a dog-eating-steak grin. My fists were clenched and every muscle in my body had come alive.

"What do you want?" I used my intimidating voice. He didn't seem to care much.

"Tock-tick, tock-tick, tockity, tockity, tick-tick." He laughed, then shuffled away from the window. He ran, if you could call it running, with a limp.

"What was that?" Andi's words were rife with fear.

I closed the curtains, then turned. Brenda had Daniel behind her. Andi stood beside them, looking ghostly white.

I wanted to make it appear that seeing the man was no big deal, so I shrugged. "Just some poor homeless guy."

"He comes near Daniel I'll put him out of his misery," Brenda said. I had no doubts about her willingness to do so.

"He's gone now. Probably harmless. I think I scared him."

Brenda stared at me. "He didn't look scared."

She was right about that. I can be intimidating when I need to be. They teach that on the football field, but the Toc-Tick man looked like he couldn't have cared less.

"Tock-Tick?" Daniel said. "Who says tock-tick?"

Sometimes Daniel acted a little older than his ten years—about a decade older. "He has some mental problems, buddy. It probably means something to him even though it doesn't mean anything to us." My heart was pounding, my muscles still ready for flight or fight, and my brain was running like a jet engine.

Andi said, "If that guy's the reason for keeping the window shades drawn at night, then the hotel clerk should have warned us. I hate being scared like that."

I still wanted to appear calm and put the others at ease, so I started clearing the dishes. I wasn't in the mood for chicken after all.

SUNRISE COULDN'T COME fast enough for me. We cleaned up the kitchen, being sure to put everything back where we got it, wiped down the counters and stovetop, and generally left the kitchen cleaner than we found it. Part of the activity was done out of simple courtesy—after all, Jewel didn't have to provide us with food or access to the kitchen but she did, begrudgingly—and partly because we didn't want to talk anymore. Talking about Brenda's decision was like sticking a hand in a hornet's nest: the hornets don't like it; neither does the owner of the hand.

Once done with the clean up, we went to bed. It was an act on my part. I doubted I'd sleep. Instead, I did what I knew I would: I lay in bed listening to every sound the old building made, and it made plenty. Every squeak made me wonder if Brenda and Daniel were sneaking away. Every bump brought images of the Tockity man sneaking into the place to murder us as we slept. I even spent a good half-hour trying to convince myself that I should sleep at the foot of the stairs so I would know if anyone came or went.

I didn't do that. Brenda was a woman who never hesitated to say or do what she thought she should, but she wouldn't take the car and leave us stranded in Newland. Besides, I had the keys.

I did get up a dozen or so times to peer out the window to see if Tockity man or something worse was messin' about. I didn't see anything. I don't know where a man like that goes in the wee hours, but I was pretty sure he went there.

I made my way to the men's shared restroom, made use of the free toothpaste and tiny toothbrush Jewel had given me, took a quick shower, dragged the comb through my hair, and slipped into yesterday's jeans and flannel shirt, then plodded back to my room to put on boat-length sneakers.

It was still early. The sun was up, but it was still in a wrestling match with the trees and hills. The scene outside my window was an epic battle of light fighting the dark. The light was winning, but it was going to be a fifteen-round match.

I like to read my Bible in the morning and the evening, but it was stowed in the car with my other gear. I checked the nightstand next to the bed, but no dice. Apparently the Gideons didn't travel this deep in the Blue Ridge Mountains.

I did, however, find a notepad and pen. I scratched out a simple note: Gone for a quick walk. Will bring luggage up when I get back. Then we eat. –Tank.

I folded the notepaper and wedged it in the jamb of the lady's bathroom. No matter how strained things were at the moment, they'd go in the room sooner or later. I had lived off and on with these two women for a while. I was sure they'd find the note soon.

I walked down the stairs expecting to find Jewel at the desk. No sign of her. No matter. We promised not to go out until the sun was up and ol' Mr. Sun was showing his face.

I unlocked the front door and walked out.

The fresh air was sweet with dew and the smell of old growth forest. For a moment, I allowed myself to believe that all was right with the world.

It wasn't.

Chapter 5

A WALK THROUGH NOWHERE LAND

I'M A PACER. By that I mean that I like to walk when I think. I pace rooms, halls, and just about anywhere, but I really enjoy a brisk stroll outside. I know an athlete should jog, but my knees and ankles complained when I did that and I like to keep them happy. Besides, I didn't bring a jogging suit, and sweating up a flannel shirt is just plain nasty.

It was quiet outside. The air was cool, bordering on cold. A breeze rolled down Main Street, picking up leaves and bits of trash and scooting them my direction. I wasn't interested in cleaning up the town; I was interested in cleaning up my thinking.

I strolled about fifty steps then picked up the pace. It felt good. Legs eager to get out of bed found a decent pace and soon I was taking in deep breaths. My lungs were having as much fun as my legs.

Of course, having never been to lovely Newland I had no idea where I was going, so I headed back the way we drove in. That would give me a chance to see more of the town. I passed a barbershop, a beauty

35

shop, hardware store, café one and café two, a bank, and just about every other kind of business you'd expect to find in a small mountain community. The storefronts were quaint but they looked untouched, as if they had been ignored for sometime. Of course, what I know about storefronts would fit in a thimble, so I didn't give it any more thought.

When I reached the end of Main Street I noticed another smaller road. It formed a T-intersection with the main drag, ran west, and looked to be uphill all the way. I couldn't see very far up the street, but I guessed that it led to a residential area. People around here had to live someplace. Walking uphill required more effort than walking flat and I needed a little more challenge. Before heading up the lane I looked at the street sign. Getting lost would be embarrassing.

It was odd. The street sign topped an ornate, black pole, the kind used for streetlights in the old parts of cities but smaller around and not as tall. The part of the sign that read "Main Street" looked okay, but the part indicating the street I was about to walk had been painted over. I could see that once it had read Elm Street but the shoddy paint job of whitewash and handmade letters read "Nowhere." I wondered what the local Chamber of Commerce thought of that—if there was a local Chamber of Commerce. I had serious doubts about that possibility.

I headed up the street, my calves informing me that uphill walking hurt more than what I had been doing. No matter, I plodded on.

The sun was still fighting for this territory. I was in shade most of the way and the shade made things cooler. Increasing my pace allowed me to create my own heat. I listened to my breathing as I hiked and then something occurred to me. This was prime bird singing time. Birds like the morning and usually spend some of their morning encouraging the sun on its daily climb in the sky. I hadn't heard a single peep, chirp, caw, or anything else.

About three-quarters of a mile up the grade I came to another street, this one perpendicular to Nowhere and parallel to Main Street. It was clearly residential. Houses, most of them small, cabin-like structures, sat on large lots of an acre or more. Some of the exteriors looked well maintained and the yards were clear of debris; others, however, looked abandoned. Fences in front of those houses looked worn and spider webs decorated the slats. Odd. One house looked ready for guests, others looked like something the Munsters would enjoy.

I felt sad for the empty houses and those who had to leave them behind. Small towns this far away from better traveled roads tended to waste away. I've always thought living in a small town like Newland would be wonderful. A great place to raise kids.

That's when something else hit me. I walked past a dozen houses that clearly had residents, but hadn't heard a single voice or, worse, a single dog bark. That made me think. I hadn't seen any dogs any where. Then I had another thought: I hadn't seen or heard any children. Of course, I told myself, I had only been in town one night so I shouldn't get too shook up over the lack of kid and dog sightings. And when I coupled that with the weird woman at the hotel and the weirder man outside the window, I knew I was letting my imagination get the best of me. That was the story I was telling myself, but I've seen too much of the strange and the dangerous to believe my own rationalizations. Truth is, I was trying to convince myself that nothing was out of the norm, but myself wasn't having anything to do with thinking.

I kept up my pace but my mind raced ahead of me. I started to feel that people were staring at me from their homes. I wondered if whatever lived in the abandoned houses was watching. Jogging was beginning to look like a good idea, but I kept myself in check. I just kept walking like I was a normal person strolling a normal street in a normal mountain community. I doubted any of that was true.

I reached the end of the street, which I guessed was the same length as Main Street. I found another crossroad, this one with the nonthreatening name of Bass Street. That was something to be thankful for.

Rounding the corner, I continued my hike down the grade to the main drag and found myself at the other end of town, just as I expected. Before going back to the hotel I crossed Main Street and made my way to the pretty little church. It was a true chapel in the woods: white clapboard siding, double hung windows with dark green trim, and a wide set of steps to the front door. A tall and pointed steeple cast a shadow on the street. The shadow of the steeple's cross fell right in the middle of the roadway. *The cross always leaves an impression.*

I doubted the preacher or the secretary would be in the building this early, but being in, or in this case *near*, a church always eased my mind and settled my heart—something I wish my friends could experience.

At first I felt the usual comfort that always came when at a church, but then I noticed something—dust. Dust on the window sills; dust on the steps—I could see my shoe prints and the prints of someone else who had been exploring the chapel—and dust on the doorknob. And not just a faint powdering. No, sir. There was enough dust to make me think the door to the chapel hadn't been opened in some time, maybe years and that was depressing to a man like me. Nothing sadder than an empty, unused church. Since I hadn't seen any other churches so far, I grew even sadder. Perhaps, the people went to church in the next town, but if Andi's research was right, and her research was always right, the next town was at least a half-hour away, maybe more on the mountain road.

I wasn't looking at a church. I was staring at a used-to-be church; a building in church clothes. I had fought fear and depression all night. This made the depression worse. So much for an uplifting walk.

I slunk back to the hotel and unpacked the car so Andi, Brenda, and Daniel could have fresh clothes and other whatnots. The way Brenda had talked last night, I'd be returning the luggage to the car later that day.

BREAKFAST AT TIFFANY'S

IT DIDN'T TAKE long for me to carry the luggage into the hotel. The others were glad to see it, Jewel Tarkington wasn't. She was standing on the first tread of the staircase. I think the little mouse was trying to keep me from taking the luggage up.

"I did a little checking for you," Jewel said. Something happened to her face as she spoke. It took me a second or two but I realized she was forcing a smile. She seemed well outta practice. "I can get you in one of two hotels up in Sugar Hill. It's pretty close. Maybe an hour's drive. I hear it's a nice place."

I set the last bit of luggage down near the others I had already retrieved from the car. Andi, Brenda, and Daniel were going to help cart the stuff up the three flights of stairs even though I said I was happy to do it. My guess is they thought I was moving too slow.

"You hear it's a nice place?" Andi said. "You've never been there?"

"Well, no, but that doesn't matter." She shifted her weight as if thinking on her feet was taxing her. "I just want you to be comfortable."

Andi wasn't buying it. "Forgive me for such a forward question Ms. Tarkington, but have you ever been out of this town?"

Jewel reminded me of a deflating balloon. "I-I don't see what that has to do with anything."

"It doesn't," Andi said, "and I hope I didn't insult you. I'm just naturally nosey. For example, I used my smart phone to find the hotel's wireless so I could check my e-mail. I couldn't find a wireless connection."

"We don't have that sort of thing."

She said it as if Andi had been talking about pornography.

"I guessed that," Andi said, "when I didn't see a computer behind the hotel desk. Everything seems to be recorded by hand."

Andi's pattern recognition superpower seemed to be in fine shape.

"I'm a little ol' fashioned."

Brenda gave me a look. She recognized the symptoms of Andi sleuthing. To my surprise, Brenda seemed interested, too. She jumped in. "I notice there are no televisions, no phones, and no radios. This place is a black hole."

"You see there," Jewel said. "That's exactly what I mean. You two are sharp ones. I can see that." I tried not to be offended at being left off the smart list. "That's why you should go on up to Sugar Hill. They have all those things and I jus' know you'll be much more comfortable."

I gotta admit, I've never seen a business person try so hard to drive business away. I began to wonder if she was running a gambling den in here or worse.

"Well, we'll talk about it," Andi said. "and we need to change clothes and freshen up. You how we women are."

I got the feeling that Jewel didn't know.

"And we need to feed my boy, here," Brenda said. "He's a monster if he misses a meal."

"No I'm not," Daniel said. Then he growled.

Funny kid.

I picked up the heaviest bags and started for the stairs. I walked faster than needed hoping she'd fear getting run over by—wait for it—a Tank. She moved and I trudged up the stairs. The others followed carrying overnight cases.

It took only a half hour for the ladies to shower and do the stuff ladies do every morning. Daniel came to my room, sat on the bed, and fired up his video game. Personally, I think my little buddy spends too much time on that game. I guess that makes me old even though I'm not. I didn't say anything. He had been through enough these last few weeks, and all that was made worse by last night's scare. I used the time to read my Bible, but I couldn't concentrate. My thoughts were bees in a bottle. African killer bees.

THIRTY-FIVE MINUTES later we were all seated in the nearest of the two cafés, a place called Tiffany's.

"Just like the movie," Andi said. "Now we can all say, we had breakfast at Tiffany's."

42

Tiffany's Café looked old on the outside and older on the inside. Tiffany herself was no spring chicken. She was short, round, sported a double chin that swayed with each step she took, and she smelled of bacon grease, burnt toast, and stale tobacco. She wore a green stripped waitress uniform with a white apron and frilly collar. I knew she was named Tiffany because she wore a name tag, the kind with a white space to write a name on. It looked like the letters and been penned a long time ago. When we walked in she had been chatting up one of the two customers in the place. She was smiling. That evaporated the moment the little brass bell at the top of the door jingled. She looked at us like we looked at the Tockity man last night.

"Charming," Brenda said. "We've gone back in time sixty years.

"Maybe it's one of those retro places," I said. "You know, like fifties diner that serves burgers and malts."

"If it is, they went out of their way to find original fixtures. Look at the booths. They have to be decades old. They have more scars, stains, and tears than I can count."

We waited for her to seat us or at least say, "Sit anywhere." That never came. She did telegraph a pretty mean scowl our way.

I sometimes work under the philosophy that forgiveness is easier to get than permission, so I sauntered over to one of the teal and white booths and squeezed onto the bench. Clearly, it had been designed for smaller folk than me. Daniel, obviously not put off by the look of the place or the owner, took the space next to me.

"Good call." I elbowed the kid. "Now the wimmin' will be able to look right into our handsome faces while they eat."

Daniel giggled. "Wimmin'."

"The trick will be keeping our breakfast down," Brenda said. She and Andi scooted onto the the opposite seat.

Anyone listening to our conversation would think we were all happy campers. We weren't. Dark clouds hovered over us. The team felt incomplete without the professor, plus Brenda's revelation about leaving the group, the scary Tockity man, and the fact that we were in a town that made us feel like we weren't wanted had us all sitting on razor blades. Of course, the fact that we had no idea why we had been sent here didn't help.

"You folks lost?" It was Tiffany. She had a three-pack-a-day voice.

"Not at all," Brenda said. "We're seated in Tiffany's café in Newland, North Carolina. Nope, not lost at all." She was getting cranky again.

"We don't get many outsiders in here."

"Maybe we can start a trend." Brenda's face portrayed an innocent spirit I knew wasn't there. It was an act for Miss Tiffany.

"You know, we're just a small town dive, but up the road—"

"—there's a nice place in Sugar Hill." Apparently Andi had caught the same sarcasm disease as Brenda. "We're here and we're hungry now."

"Breakfast for breakfast," Daniel said.

Tiffany looked puzzled. I tried to explain. "We had breakfast for dinner last night at the hotel."

"You stayed in town last night?"

"Yes, ma'am," I said. I figured one of the adults needed to be polite.

"At Jewel's place?"

"Yes, ma'am. She let us use the kitchen."

Tiffany's face hardened. "She did, did she?"

"Yes, ma'am. I could really use some coffee. We all could." I needed to change the subject before Brenda got in the woman's face. "Except the boy, of course. Do you have milk?"

"We have milk. I still think—"

I could see Andi tense. Andi was sweet and smart and kind but she had limits. I was pretty sure Tiffany was about to cross into the danger zone.

"Excuse me, ma'am," Andi said. "I sometimes get things wrong but it seems you don't want to serve us. Could that be because one of us is black? I'm sure that's not it, but if it were, we would have to let someone know that Tiffany's is still practicing segregation."

Tiffany drew herself up as tall as she could. "Of course not. I ain't got no problem with a person's color. Like I said, we just don't get new people in town and when we do, they have the good sense to keep moving."

"Now that sounds like a threat." Andi was pulling out all the stops. I had no doubt she was spoiling for a fight. Too many pent up emotions can make people a little crazy.

"No threat, darlin'. I'm just telling you the Gospel truth."

I've read the Gospels many times, and I'm sure she wasn't using the word the way the Bible does.

Andi stared at her with innocence on her face and laser beams in her eyes.

45

Tiffany sighed. "Coffee for three and milk for your boy." She was speaking to me.

"He's not my son," I said. "He's my little buddy."

The woman looked at Andi who shook her head slowly.

"Daniel's my son," Brenda said.

Tiffany looked at Daniel's white face then at Brenda's black skin. We get that a lot.

"I'll get the coffee then take your order."

She walked away. The other two diners stared at us. I sized them up. Both looked to be well into their sixties and in no way a threat. I also noted the cook had come out. He was twice as round as Tiffany and sported the same double chin and dingy clothes.

"Girl," Brenda said, "did you just play the race card?"

"I don't know what you're talking about." The slight grin on Andi's face told me she was lying.

Brenda beamed. It was good to see a smile on her face, even if it only lasted a moment.

Tiffany brought the coffee and a milk for Daniel, we ordered, and she trudged off. I used the time to bring the girls up to date about my walk. It was a short story, but they recognized the weirdness in it. There wasn't much to discuss, but at least they were up to speed.

The food arrived quickly. I guess Tiffany felt the sooner we ate the sooner we'd leave. I dug into a Denver omelet, Andi had a bowl of oatmeal, Brenda had scrambled eggs and hash browns. Daniel wasted no time getting to his pancakes. We ate in silence for a few minutes, then Brenda asked the question we've all been waiting for: "What are the odds of getting me and Daniel to the Asheville airport?"

I didn't answer. I didn't want to answer. I had been hoping that Brenda would change her mind. Considering the picture she had drawn, I was pretty sure she wouldn't. She wasn't concerned with her safety; she was worried about Daniel. So was I.

Andi broke the silence. "Since we don't know why we're here, I can't think of a reason not to leave. It's not like our mysterious, invisible handlers have given us any direction. Telling us where to go and funding our trip, putting money in our bank accounts to live on so we can be on call isn't enough. Every situation we walked into we walked into blind. If they want our help, our gifts, then they should give us more than crumbs to follow."

"Amen to that," Brenda said.

I wanted to argue the point, but I had no material to use. Everything Andi said was true. We are sent places, bizarre things happen, we get sucked in, we fight for our lives and the lives of others, then nothing. We don't anything about those who send us and fund us. We know they clean up after us, or so it seems. That's it.

"Well, Cowboy?" Brenda was pummeling me with her eyes. "I can drive if you want. I know how to do that."

"I know. I just don't want to lose you and Daniel."

I know it's not possible, but I felt my heart melt. She was leaving to protect Daniel. I was being selfish by resisting her. "I'll load up the car as soon as we're done eating."

Brenda's expression softened. "Thanks, Bjorn. You da man."

"Tank's da man," Daniel said.

Then he sat bolt upright. He looked up and to the area of the door we walked through a short time before. The he snapped his head around, seeing things only he could see. "Uh oh."

I didn't like Daniel's tone. Too much fear in it.

"What, buddy?" I stared at him.

He didn't answer with words. Instead, he snatched the fork from my hand then gathered up all the silverware.

"Daniel, what are you doing?" Brenda sounded both irked and frightened at the same time.

He shoved his plate to the floor, then proceeded to do the same with everyone else's plates and cups. The racket hurt my ears.

"Hey! You're gonna pay for that." Tiffany started our way. I saw the cook come out from the back.

If Daniel was just some other kid; if I hadn't seen him in action before; if we hadn't seen so many unexplainable things; then people would be right to think he was throwing a tantrum. I knew better.

"Hold on," Daniel said clutching the silverware to his chest. Then his head snapped to the side as he directed his gaze out the window. I followed his example. "Tock-Tick."

Just outside the window was the Tockity man. The same disheveled, ratty looking, homeless guy. The same freaky eye patch.

He was grinning again, exposing what few teeth he had left.

Through the glass I heard him say, "Tock-tick, tock-tick, Tockity-tick-tick."

Tiffany's voice sounded a mile or two away. "What's he doing in the daylight—"

Then the world went white.

There was pain.
There was fear.
Then there was nothing but white.

Chapter 7

I DON'T THINK WE'RE IN KANSAS ANYMORE

ONCE, ON THE football field, back when I was playing on a junior college team (before I transferred to the University of Washington and made a hash of that), I put a wicked tackle on a running back. I got the worst of the deal. I couldn't breathe and my head felt like a team of workers were trying to knock a hole in my skull using sledgehammers. It was my first and only concussion. One is enough.

When the white went away, I felt the same. I struggled to open my eyes and had to focus just to breathe. The air tasted funny. The light seemed a shade or two off from where it had been. It took less than a second for me to stop thinking about myself and start thinking of the others. With eyes now wide, I looked first at Daniel. He looked pale, slightly green, and more than a little stunned. He clutched the silverware to his chest. He had missed one—a butter knife that Brenda had been using. I found it stuck deep in the backrest of the booth between

Daniel and me. Daniel had saved us from becoming pincushions—or silverware cushions.

Andi was in her spot, her hands on the edge of the table as if pushing herself back. Her sometimes wild red hair was wild again. "What . . . was . . . that?"

Brenda looked ready to upchuck her breakfast. Her mouth hung open and she gulped for air like a fish tossed on the dock.

"Are you choking?" I feared her mouth might have been full of food when whatever happened, happened.

She shook her head. I knew what the problem was. I've experienced it a few times; many football players have. She had had all the wind knocked out of her. Her diaphragm was in a spasm. It's a lousy feeling. I reached across the table and put my hand on the side of her head. "Look at me."

She didn't.

"Brenda, look at me. Right in the eyes."

She did. Those eyes were growing wider.

"Relax. Just look at me and relax. Your breath will come back. Just give it a moment."

I rubbed my thumb on her cheek. Andi slipped an arm around her.

Then Brenda inhaled deeply—and noisily. She sounded like someone who had gone down with a ship and just made the long swim to the surface.

"There it is. There it is." I continued to stroke her cheek. "Keep looking at me. There ya' go." Another deep inhalation. Another noisy gasp. "Stay relaxed. You're doing great."

It took a minute or two before she was breathing in a normal fashion.

"Can you speak now?" That would tell me that her airway was clear and everything was working as it should.

She spoke. I won't tell you what she said because it would earn an R-rating. I've been around football jocks all my life and those boys know how to swear. Nonetheless, Brenda could give lessons.

She spoke again. "I don't ever want to do that again."

I lowered my hand. "Me neither."

"Cowboy, you healed me. Thanks."

I mentioned earlier that we all have our own special gifts. Andi sees patterns, Brenda draws the future, Daniel sees angels, and I can heal people. Well, *sometimes*. It doesn't work every time. In fact, I never know if it's going to work or not. You can imagine how frustrating that is. If I had full control of that gift, I'd spend my days walking through hospitals putting doctors out of work—if you know what I mean.

"Glad to help, but it wasn't me."

She raised a hand— "I know. You think it was God."

"Well, that too, but I don't think I healed you. You just had the wind knocked out of you. All you needed was a little time for your breathing to reset itself."

"Is that all. I thought I was dying."

"Me too," Daniel said.

I took a moment to gather my thoughts and tame my emotions when I saw it. I glanced around Tiffany's, or what used to be Tiffany's. "Um guys . . ."

They saw me casting my gaze this way and that. While we were blinded by the bright white light someone had snuck into Tiffany's and repainted the walls. They also added a dozen customers, and changed Tiffany's uniform. Except it wasn't Tiffany. The lady moving from table to table filling coffee cups and joking with the patrons was painfully thin, had short black hair, looked to be in her twenties, and stood close to six feet tall if she were an inch.

Other things had changed. In the place we had just been, Tiffany brought us menus. Here the menus were held in a wire holder. I grabbed one. Brenda and Andi did the same.

"This ain't good." Brenda was right.

"This can't be." Andi kept her gaze fixed to the menu. Her eyes darted back and forth. "I-I can't read this."

"Nothin' wrong with your eyes, girlfriend." Brenda touched the printing on the menu as if she could absorb its meaning through her fingertips. "I can't make heads or tales of it, myself."

I had noticed the same thing. There were plenty of words but they were written in some other language. Something tickled my brain. It looked familiar— "The scroll!"

I said that a little too loud. Several people turned to face us. Worse, the waitress came over. I didn't see how that could be a good thing.

Andi nodded. "That's where I've seen these letters." She paused just a moment then asked, "Am I the only one who feels like we just made some kind of trip?"

I wanted to say more, but the waitress arrived. She said—something. I have no idea what. Her tone was light and sing-songy. No anger. She did, however, look a little puzzled. I glanced at Andi and Brenda and they looked as lost as I felt. Andi shrugged. Brenda shook her head. She pointed at a particular item on the menu. That made me wonder what happened to the breakfast we had just eaten when we were in Tiffany's. The silverware had made it but not the dirty dishes Daniel had pushed on the floor. That was fine with me. I don't know how I'd explain that. Of course, I didn't know how to explain any of this.

Reaching deep in my gut I brought out what I felt was a pretty convincing smile and held up one index finger. I hoped the universal, "Give me a sec" sign would be, well, universal. "Could we have another moment?"

Daniel cranked his head my direction. Brenda slapped her forehead. Andi sat still and looked like I had just undressed in front of everyone. The waitress cocked her head. That's when I realized, in my infinite wisdom, that if I couldn't understand her, she couldn't understand me. I had just proved that we weren't from around these parts.

She studied me for a moment, nodded, and walked away.

"I'm an idiot." I squeezed my eyes shut as if that would back the clock up. It didn't.

"Anyone want to argue with him?" Brenda said.

Andi, who normally was kind said, "Not me."

"Now that the cat is out of the bag, what do we do?" Brenda said.

"We need to go somewhere where we can talk." Andi reached for the small purse she carried. "I don't think it's wise to stay here."

"What if what just happened happens again?" The washing machine in my head was set to high speed. "If we move from this spot and the thing happens again, then we'll miss our ride back to our world."

"We can't sit here doing nothing." Andi looked around the café. "People are staring."

I glanced around again. She was right. We had become the morning's entertainment. "Okay, you win. I don't have any better ideas." To Daniel I said, "Scoot on out, buddy. We're gonna blow this popsicle stand."

He set the silverware down and wiggled out of the booth. I slid across the seat. Brenda and Andi were already out and watched me try to work my bulk out of a booth made for thin people.

"Uh oh," Brenda whispered. "Heads up."

The waitress walked in our direction again. I couldn't help noticing that she was looking at us, then looking at the door. At first I thought she was going to block our way out. Then I noticed what she had already noticed. A yellow-and-white sedan had pulled to the side of the street. It had some lettering over a round symbol on the doors. On the top of the car was a globe about the size of a large softball.

"Guys . . ." I nodded out the window. The others turned just in time to see two men get out of the front seat. They wore matching green uniforms. There were yellow patches sewn to their sleeves near the shoulder. My Uncle Bart is the sheriff of Dickerson County in Oregon so I know a cop car when I see one. And I was seeing one.

"Nuts." It was the best I could manage.

The skinny waitress opened the door and I was pretty sure she wasn't opening it for us. I was wrong. She smiled. Bowed her head for a moment and waved us out.

Out we went.

The officers were there to greet us, and I mean *greet* us. Both smiled. Both dipped their heads in a slight bow, then the older of the two extended his hand. He either wanted to shake hands or was taking a sneaky approach to clamp on the business end of handcuffs.

It was the former. I extended my hand and he took hold of my wrist, smiling all the time. Just as I was beginning to think the guy was going to twist my arm behind my back, cuff and search me, he gave my wrist a friendly squeeze and shake. I took his wrist and did the same. That broadened his smile. A second later, the junior officer instigated the same kind of greeting. Then they moved to Andi and Brenda. The older of the two mussed Daniel's hair. Just for the record, Daniel hates that. He didn't say anything but I know the kid well enough to know he was restraining himself.

I did a quick survey of the sedan. It was a cop car, all right. It had something that looked like a shotgun vertically mounted to the dash, and a wire partition between the front and rear seat.

People moved along the walkway, most shot us a glance and smiled. A few even waved.

"I gotta say it," Andi said, "but I don't think we're in Kansas anymore, Toto."

Even I caught the reference to *The Wizard of Oz* movie. Unlike Dorothy, however, this world looked very much like the one we left, except there were more people, it looked cleaner, and folk were friendly.

"Unbelievable," Brenda said. "A half-hour ago we were planning on going back to the Asheville airport."

"I've got a feeling that it's a longer drive now," Andi said.

"Much longer," I said.

LITTLEFOOT, NEW AND IMPROVED

WHEN WE WALKED out of the café (the waitress actually said, "Thank you for coming," as we exited), I wondered how they were going to get three grown adults (in my case, overgrown) and a ten-year-old boy into the yellow-and-white patrol car along with two police officers. The car was the size of a Prius. I started to ask the officers, but it would do no good. Even if they understood me, I wouldn't understand them.

My question was answered a moment later when another patrol car pulled up. It did so casually. No siren, no red or blue emergency lights—or in this case, green and yellow lights. It took a second for me to realize that the car made almost no noise as it pulled to the curb. I heard the tires on the pavement, but no engine. Electric? That was my guess.

Two additional officers exited the car. They wore the same yellow and brown uniform as the first two. They approached, each with a wide grin on his face. The older looking one—I made him to be in his thirties and his partner in his twenties—approached me and shook my hand like a fan meeting his favorite movie star. I half-expected him to pull out an autograph book. He did more than shake my hand, he pumped it. He then moved to Andi and Brenda, greeting them in the same way. We did another round of handshaking with the younger officer.

To say I was confused would be downplaying what I felt. We were in a town nearly identical to Newland but different enough to make my head spin. I once read that someone asked Daniel Boone if he had ever been lost in the woods. He said, "No, but I've been bewildered for a couple of weeks." I was that kind of bewildered.

"I'm not leaving Daniel!"

Brenda had pulled the boy to her side. The officer looked at one another. Their faces revealed their confusion.

"What's wrong?" I asked her.

"I think they want to separate us."

I've seen that angry face too many times to not notice it now. One of the officers caught my eye then pointed at Daniel, then Andi.

"Ah, I get it." I moved to Brenda and Daniel. I put my hand on Daniel's shoulder then moved it to Brenda's. I did that three times. The officers looked at Brenda, then Daniel, then Andi. Andi caught on. She put one hand on the side of each of their shoulders and pushed them together. There wasn't much movement involved since Brenda already held Daniel close.

Then Andi surprised me—she stepped to my side and took hold of my arm, like we were a couple. That was the first good thing to happen to me that day. As far as I was concerned, Andi could hang onto me as long as she liked. I wouldn't complain a bit.

The first officer we met opened the back door of the police car and motioned for us to enter. Clearly, he didn't mean all of us. A quick glance told me that one of the policemen had opened the back door of the other patrol car.

"You go with Brenda and Daniel," I told Andi.

"I don't need her protection," Brenda said.

"It's not you I'm worried about." I looked at the two officers by the first car.

"You're a funny man, Tank. A real gut-buster." She climbed into the back of the car and Daniel followed.

"You're right, I'd better ride with them." Andi released my arm and the world seemed to dim a little.

It only took a few steps to reach the second car and I climbed in. I've never been in the back of a police car, but as I said, I've been in my Uncle Bart's sheriff's patrol vehicle; always in the front seat. This car was clean as could be. It didn't smell, the interior looked like it had just rolled off the factory floor. It's good to be thankful for small things, especially when you've been transported to some unknown place. So I was thankful.

A few moments later we were moving down the street, the car purring like a content kitty. What puzzled me now was where they could be taking us. Most of this town was a dead ringer for Newland, North Carolina. Newland was small. My hike earlier led me through town and up into some of the residential streets. In Newland, the sheriff's office was a storefront. It didn't seem to be the kind of place with fancy electric cars and at least four officers on duty.

So the place was similar, but not the same. With that realization I began to think of this place as New Land.

They drove us out of New Land and I hoped we didn't have an hour's drive to the next town—Sugar Hill, it was called in Newland. For all I knew, there was no Sugar Hill; or it could be a major city. Nothing would surprise me now.

The drive turned out to be short, which was a relief. About ten minutes out of town, up a winding road, was a large, modern-looking building. It reminded me of an office complex and maybe it was.

Brenda, Daniel, and Andi were already out of the car when my chauffeur stopped the car. One of the cops had to open the door for me since it couldn't be opened from the inside. At least that was the same as the cop cars back home.

We were escorted to and through a large glass front and glass doors that opened as we neared. If this was a local police station, then it had to be the fanciest one I'd ever seen.

Inside, was a large lobby with a fountain in the middle. A statue stood in the center of the fountain. It was a sculpture of a policeman in uniform and utility belt. In one arm he held a child, and with the other arm extended, he pointed the way. The way to what? I don't know. Safety? The future? A donut shop? My Uncle Bart would have my head for that last thought.

I stepped next to Andi, hoping she'd take my arm again—she didn't—and Brenda. They and Daniel were staring at the statue.

"Cheesy," Daniel said.

That made Brenda chuckle and I was glad we were the only ones who could understand him.

We had waited for about thirty seconds when a man in a fancy uniform with some in-your-face decorations on the shoulders and sleeves approached. He looked to be in his early sixties. His hair was the color of polished silver, and his wrinkles were deep, no doubt earned by a life in law enforcement. Like his officers before him, he beamed, shook our hands, and treated us like foreign dignitaries.

He spoke to us, but I understood none of it. He could have been giving me sport scores for all I could tell. Then he gave me a slap on the shoulder. I took that to mean that he had said something nice, or maybe funny.

He motioned for us to follow him. I noticed that the officers who brought us here didn't follow. Apparently they had done their job. That also told me that the chief—that's what I assumed the older man to be—felt we were no threat to him.

The rest of the building is a bit of a blur. I tried to take everything in but it was all a little overwhelming. Questions buzzed in my brain looking for answers and they were coming up short.

"Anyone got a guess about what happened?" Brenda spoke softly.

"Not a clue," Andi said. "I could give a dozen guesses and be wrong on every count."

Brenda looked at Daniel and her mood darkened. "Batman and Robin. We should have moved on when the lady at the hotel told us."

"You think she knows something?" I asked.

"That'd be my guess."

The chief's office was spacious and dominated by a power desk with photos, file folders, and a cup half-filled with what I assumed was coffee.

There was something else in the room. I should say there was *someone* else in the room: a woman. She had long blond hair that was parted down the middle and hypnotic brown eyes. She looked to be in her twenties and wore a green pants suit. She stood. She was tall and gorgeous.

"Hello, Tank," she said. She said it in English.

"You know me?"

"Of course I do, silly. How could I forget you?" Her smile was dazzling.

"I'm sorry, ma'am, I think I'd remember you if we had met before." I couldn't say why at the moment, but I felt like an idiot, like the last person in the room to get the punchline of a joke.

She smiled again. If her smile was any brighter I would need sunglasses. Then she did something weird: she took off her shoes and wiggled her toes.

Still nothing.

I heard her give a playful sigh as she closed her eyes. When she opened them I was staring at the same face but a different pair of eyes: green eyes. Something in my brain came out of hibernation. She closed her lids again, then opened them so we could see what a lovely shade of blue they were.

"Wait."

Daniel charged forward and wrapped his arms around her.

Andi clapped her hands. "Hello, Helsa."

"Helsa?" The thing that woke up in my brain got busy. I got it. I didn't understand it, but I got it.

"Littlefoot!"

It was my turn to embrace her and she embraced me back. When we parted, I asked the obvious. "I don't get it. When I last saw you were just a child."

"That was a long time ago, Tank."

That confused me. "It was less than a year ago."

"It's been a little longer here."

Now I was getting a headache.

Helsa's voice turned dark. "We have a lot to discuss."

"You got that right," Brenda said. "You can start by telling us how to get home from here."

I didn't like the look on Helsa's face.

FEW ANSWERS, TOO MANY QUESTIONS

AFTER THE HUGGING was done, we sat so we could chat. I wasn't sure how to feel. To say I was confused wouldn't be going far enough. I first met Helsa (her name means *devoted to God* in Hebrew—of course her name just *sounds* like Hebrew, as far as we could figure) when our team was just getting its legs. It was our fourth adventure, and not all that long ago. Some days it seems a decade back. And back then, she was less than ten years old.

I'll keep this short. I mentioned my Uncle Bart, the county sheriff, in an area that included Dickerson, Oregon. Every year I go up to Oregon to watch the Rose Bowl with him and his family. While there, he got a call to investigate strange footprints in the snow of a farmer's field. He asked me to go with him and I did. We found footprints all right. Small ones. Prints of a barefoot child walking through the snow. That image still haunts me.

We found the little girl and she was as cute as a button. Didn't talk, but she did carry a scroll with strange lettering. That's what Andi recognized back in the café.

"I hope everyone has been well." Helsa was smiling when she said that but the smile evaporated pretty quick. "Where's the professor?"

"That's hard to say," Andi said.

"He's dead." Brenda didn't mince words. "Police say he committed suicide."

Some people grieve with endless tears. Brenda shed a few of those when she didn't think people were watching. Some people grieve with anger. That was more Brenda's speed.

"There's a lot of doubt about that." Andi's tone wasn't cold, but it was pretty chilly. "Things don't add up. He was looking for a way to access alternate dimensions." She paused and looked at Brenda. "And look where we are: a different universe."

I'm not used to being the reasonable one, but I needed to give it a go. "The whole thing has been a little hard on us, Helsa."

"Either way, he's not with you." Helsa's face darkened with sadness and her eyes changed color to a pale gray. "It's a loss. I liked him. I felt nothing but love from him."

"That makes you the lucky one," Brenda said. The professor had always been toughest on Brenda. He had a difficult time being anything but analytical.

"I only got to spend a short time with him and I had become a child by then."

"This stuff gives me a headache."

To Brenda's credit, she looked like her head hurt.

Andi's curiosity was taking over. I can't say she was as brilliant as the professor, but given the chance, I think she could be. Nothing gets by the girl.

"When we first met you, you couldn't or wouldn't speak. Now you handle English better than Tank. How is that?"

"Hey." It was all I could say.

"No offense." Andi smiled at me and all was right with the world—whatever world this was.

"Come on." Helsa stood. "I'll show you."

We stood, too.

"But first I need to warn you. It might be a little upsetting."

"Cool, just what we need: something else to upset us." I probably don't need to tell you that Brenda said that.

Helsa talked as we walked. "I picked up a few things from you, but I've been studying the language ever since."

"They teach English here?" Andi said.

"No. Not at all. But when the Others arrive, I try to learn their language."

That confused me. "Others?"

"That's what you are. You're not from our world, so people here think of you as the Others. That's not bad. My people love the Others—mostly.

She filled us in on how she was a quick study and that English was a simple enough language. I was born in the good ol' U.S. of A. and I don't find English, proper English, all that easy.

"Some of our team has visited your universe and brought back books for us to study."

"Team?" Andi asked.

"Yes." Helsa slowed to a stop in the wide hallway we had been strolling through. "You know there are other teams, don't you?"

"Wait, wait, wait." Brenda pinched the bridge of her nose as if it would clarify everything. "There are other people like us?"

"Yes. Of course."

"Doing the same thing we do?"

"Again, yes." Helsa looked puzzled, as if this should be common knowledge taught in grade schools. "Not in your universe. You are unique. I'm sure you know that. Only you can do what you do."

I felt good hearing that, but I had serious doubts that Brenda got the same thrill.

"You know, old man McKinney tried to dial us in on the whole extra-dimensions and multiple universes thing, but he just confused me."

"You don't want to go to anyplace that has more or less dimensions. Nothing would make sense. There are many universes in the greater cosmos. You're in my universe now; I was in yours for a short time. The people you battle are from a universe different from yours or mine."

"The Gate," I said. "We call them the Gate."

"They have many names; most of them less kind."

"They don't deserve kindness," Brenda said.

No one wanted to argue the point.

"No, they don't." Helsa lowered her head and seemed to sink deeper in sadness. "They are smarter, have a better understanding of these things, and use more powerful equipment. They mean your world great harm."

"We gathered that." Andi had had several close calls with death because of our work. I figure that gave her the right to be snippy.

Helsa stopped and turned to us. "How much do you know about...the people who are helping you fight the Gate?"

"Next to nothing." I offered that bit of revelation. I've noticed that as a group we don't much care to reveal our ignorance. Not many people take me seriously, so I don't mind admitting to not knowing things I should know.

Andi offered more information. "They only contact us through e-mail. They pay for our travels and our bank accounts go up every month, not enough to make us rich, but enough that we don't have to get jobs to survive. They don't talk to us; they just send us tickets to fly or directions to drive to some location. They never tell us the whys and wherefores. They also seem to clean up after us."

"Clean up?" Helsa raised an eyebrow.

"How do I explain this?" Andi furrowed her brow. "We've endured some strange things: killer fungus, creatures that swim in the fog and eat pedestrians, flying orbs—it's a long list. Yet somehow, most of it is kept out of the media. I don't know how they do it, but when we ride off into the sunset, they send in the janitors."

Helsa nodded.

"I'm afraid we don't know any more than you. I hate to admit that. I wish I could sit you down and tell you everything you need to know and answer all your questions. I can't. I'm just as confused as you.

I'm part of a team here, and what you describe is the same as what we experience."

"You're part of a team?" I couldn't believe what I heard.

"Yes, Tank. It is why I was sent to your universe, to your world. It is why I'm here now. I think it is why *you're* are here now. We need you."

She sighed from deep in her soul, then started down the corridor. I had a bazillion questions but didn't ask them. Helsa had something to show us and she was intent on doing so right now. We fell in line and followed her as she led us to another wing of the building. I noticed the doors had numbers and many had lights over the door. It reminded me of a hospital. Then it hit me. It *was* a hospital. At least a hospital wing.

Helsa stopped at a pair of doors. A sign was mounted to each of the doors, signs I couldn't read, but—if I were a betting man—I would wager they read NO ADMITTANCE. A phone hung next to the doors. Amazing how many things were the same in our two worlds, universes, or whatever. The phone looked like the wall-mounted variety back home, but was the color of Red Vines candy and slightly smaller than I would have expected. She said something into the phone that was just as mysterious to me as the words on the sign.

The doors swung open and Helsa walked through. "Brace yourself."

I hate it when someone says that.

I led the others in. They seemed a little hesitant after Helsa's warning.

The place smelled of old people. The air was a mix of antiseptic, urine, skin lotion. The room reminded me of an ICU unit, except the patients didn't have private rooms. I guess it was more of a ward than anything else. Nurses, dressed in blue uniforms, moved from bed to bed. There were, by my estimation, forty or so souls there. I could only guess at the ages of people. Some looked to be in their early sixties, others looked well beyond the century mark.

For a moment I was certain I had just walked into a sci fi movie. IV bags hung from metal stands. Some of the patients had fluid flowing into them from more than one IV bag and the fluids were different colors. It looked as if they were getting a transfusion of rainbow juice.

The patients were quiet. The heart monitors were also silent. Soft music drifted from the ceiling and sounded like something a classical composer would create. I scanned the room, then I focused on the patients. Each wore a yellow patient gown; each person had deep wrinkles plowed by years of life.

A thought wormed its way into my brain. Morgues were places where they kept dead people. This seemed like a morgue for the almost dead. A chill spread through me, freezing me from the inside out. A glance at the girls told me the scene had the same effect on them. Andi was pale. Brenda found something on the floor to look at. Daniel was different. He kept his head up and strolled to an elderly lady reclined in a hospital bed. Her hair was a flat silver, her skin the color of parchment.

He smiled. She smiled back. It reminded me of two children meeting for the first time and becoming friends. The kid took her hand. The sight of it filled me with huge pride. It almost brought me to tears. My breath caught. My eyes burned.

My heart went out to the old woman in the bed. She clung to a child's doll. She held it up for Daniel to see, then wiggled it so the doll seemed to dance. Just like a child would do. Then the old woman giggled. The giggle was as light as a feather and floated like one through the room. I glanced around the place again and noticed that several of the old folks had a child's toy on the bed with them. The woman giggled again and she sounded just like a little girl—

My stomach contracted into a knot. My knees shook and gave up their strength. I bent forward and fought an almost irresistible urge to vomit on the clean, high-polished floor.

"Oh, dear God." I said that so softly that I was surprised to learn that Andi and Brenda heard it.

A hand on my shoulder. "Tank, what's wrong?" I didn't have to look to know it was Andi's hand.

I raised a finger, straightened. Took two deep breaths and walked from the room. Andi and Brenda followed; Daniel did not.

"Tank. Talk to me." Andi was by my side. Brenda stood a few feet in front of me.

I stumbled back a few steps until my back touched the corridor wall, then my legs decided to quit. I slid to the floor.

Brenda tried a more direct approach to get my attention. "Cowboy, so help me if you don't start talking I'm gonna hit you so hard your grandparents will scream."

"Is it the old people?" Andi said.

I tilted my head up. "They're not old. They're . . . they're young! Dear God, they're kids! Children!"

THE FOUNTAIN OF ELDERLINESS

HELSA BROUGHT A cup of black fluid that I assumed was coffee. I know coffee and this wasn't it. I drank it anyway, hoping it would put the steel back in my spine.

"You understand?" Helsa sat beside me. We were in the cafeteria. In the corner. Far from the police officers, nurses, doctors, and other people who worked in this place.

"I don't," Andi said.

"Me, neither." Brenda sounded irritated again. "Someone better start talkin' or I'm gonna lose my kind and gentle reputation."

"Tell me I'm wrong, Helsa. For the love of God, tell me I'm wrong."

She sat in the chair next to me and took my hand. "I can't."

After a deep breath, Helsa looked at Andi, Brenda, and Daniel. "What do you remember of my visit to your world?"

Andi rose to the bait. "You were a kid. Your eyes changed color there as they do here—"

"Younger," Daniel said. "You got younger."

Helsa nodded. "That's right."

A few seconds passed and Brenda began to swear. I think she used every profanity she knew. Andi sat like a statue for a few moments, then asked, "So these are kids from our world? How long have they been here?"

"The ones in that room have been on this side—in our universe—for about two weeks. A few longer; a few shorter."

"How do they end up here?"

"We're not sure. Probably the same way you did."

"Can't you send them back?"

"We've tried . . . we would if we could."

Andi never shied away from asking tough questions. Apparently the steel in my spine had moved to her. "How--" She stopped, then took another running start at the question. "How old was the person Daniel was talking to?"

Helsa had to reach deep for the answer. She pursed her lips, blinked several times, then, "Eight."

"Eighty?" Brenda jumped in. "You said 'eighty,' right?"

"No. Eight years old. Many have already died of old age. The older they are when they get here, the faster they age."

I braced myself for another barrage of curses but it never came. Instead, Brenda leaned forward and covered her face. She reminded me of a deflated balloon.

My turn to ask the difficult question: "How long before we begin to change?"

Helsa gave my hand a squeeze. "It's already started."

One more question from me, but I was already sure of what I was going to hear. "Where are the adults that came over?"

Helsa wasn't the kind to soft peddle things. "Dead."

WHEN A PERSON hears something that doesn't make much sense, it's only natural to call it nonsense and get back to life. That was my first reaction, but ever since I pushed together with my friends I'd seen so many things that didn't make sense that I lost my ability to be surprised. Hearing that we would grow old quickly just like Helsa grew younger when she was in our universe was unwelcome news. I wanted to call it nonsense, but I couldn't. Truth was, I was already feeling a little older, but I figured that was due to an already tough day.

There wasn't much conversation after that. Helsa asked us to tell her all the details of what had happened in Newland before we were hijacked outta our own world. She was so different from the little girl I used to call Littlefoot. Clearly her mind was running at top speed; me, not so much.

Food arrived—at least we didn't have to stand in line and fill our own plates—I was ready to dig in. It looked familiar. There were mashed potatoes on my plate, but they weren't white. They weren't the color of sweet potatoes, either. To me they looked gray, like they had been left in the field too long. I'm not a picky eater so I gave it a taste. It was glorious. Slightly sweet. Still, they were gray potatoes. Also on the plate were string beans, and thank the good

Lord, they were the right shade of green. A nice salad of greens was nestled beside the beans. I usually think of salads as rabbit food, but I had been taught to eat what was on my plate. There were other things, none of which looked like meat. So I asked.

"I should have mentioned this earlier." Helsa grinned. "No one eats meat here."

"You're all vegetarians?" I felt like a man who had just been robbed.

"Yes. We don't kill animals for food."

I looked at Andi who seemed fine with the revelation. I glanced at Daniel, he looked distracted and didn't care about what he ate—and I've seen the kid down his fair share of hot dogs and hamburgers. Then there was Brenda. I studied her as she studied the stuff on her plate. She looked ready to cut her wrists.

"We gotta find a way home," Brenda said.

Helsa let us eat then said, "You mentioned a crazy man at the kitchen window of the hotel and the restaurant."

"Yes, probably just some homeless guy. He had some issues."

"He was crazier than an outhouse rat." Brenda didn't bother looking up from her plate. Her description was a tad cruel, but I couldn't argue with it.

"Tockity man," Daniel said. He hadn't done much talking of late, especially since we left the hospital ward. He had that distant look in his eyes. Something was working in the kid's brain.

"Tockity man?" Helsa asked.

"It was something he said— "

"Ranted." Andi wasn't bothered by the food and had made some good headway into cleaning her plate.

I carried on. "Both times we saw him, he said, 'Tock-tick, tock-tick, tockity, tockity, tick-tick.' He got some of the words backwards. Andi's right. The man was raving."

"And he had an eye-patch?"

"Yep. Hand made job. Cut it out of a Corn Flakes box and tied it on with a string."

"He didn't get the words backwards," Helsa said. "That line is from a children's poem." She closed her eyes then spoke as if reading words printed on the inside of her eyelids:

"Tock, tock, tock goes the clock,
Tick, tick, tick, the hands make their pick.
Around the face the hands do move;
Our work the heart does prove.
Tock-tick, tock-tick,
Tockity, tockity, tick-tick,
What life will you pick?"

Andi looked puzzled. "I see your children's poems are as confusing and unsettling as ours."

"It is very old, and I'm translating into your language so it doesn't sound the same aloud as it does in my head. It meant more two-hundred years ago than it does today. I haven't heard it since I was a child. I mean a child in my world."

"Sick minds are attracted to sick ideas," Brenda said. "I once did a tat on a guy that was nothing more than, 'And down will come Baby.'"

"You mean like the line in Rock-a-Bye Baby?" I always hated that lullaby.

"Yes. There are variations of the song, but most describe a baby in a cradle, hung in a tree and when the wind blows it rocks the cradle, then it mentions the bough—the tree limb—breaks, the baby and cradle fall."

Helsa leaned back as if Andi's word came with a stench. "That's horrible."

"No one would argue with you," Andi said.

"Mothers still sing it to their babies without knowing what they're singing." Brenda's grumpiness had moved up a level.

I decided to get the conversation back on track. "So why would Tockity Man say those words to us?"

Helsa shrugged. "I don't know. It's the first I've heard of him . . ." She trailed off and that made my antennas go up. "Unless . . ."

"Unless what?" I was desperate for answers.

"I need to check on a few things." Helsa stood. "You should rest. You've had a challenging day."

"Challenging?" Brenda said. "That's one word for it."

Helsa patted Brenda on the shoulder. To my relief, she pulled her hand back without a single bite mark. "Brenda, you are important."

She said nothing more, but pivoted and walked from the cafeteria.

USELESS HANDS

HELSA SENT SOMEONE to show us our rooms, which were in the same building. They reminded me of dorm rooms. My room had a wide bed, a dresser, a small desk, a closet, and a bathroom. I made use of the latter, then stripped down and tried to make use of the bed. The mattress was firm, just the way I liked it. I needed sleep. Nothing is more taxing on mind and body than over-the-top emotions, and my mind and body had had it. The oblivion of sleep was what I wanted.

I was to be deprived. Although the bed was comfortable, my back ached, my stomach was sour, and my brain was doing jumping jacks. Every time I closed my eyes, images flashed on the movie screen of my brain: images of Brenda talking about the Batman syndrome, pictures of the Tockity man standing at the hotel and the café window, and—this was the worst of all—a memory of the children dressed in old bodies, slowly dying in the hospital wing.

I stared at the ceiling through the dim light provided by thick curtains. Something warm and wet trickled down the sides of my face. Children. When that realization hit me, I considered it the worst blow I had ever received. My insides quivered; my brain became Jell-O, and I was feeling the same way again.

It took me awhile to admit it, but I was wrestling with a different problem, one that embarrasses me to admit. As I mentioned, each member of the team has a spiritual gift. That's my phrase for it. Brenda *sometimes* draws the future; Andi *often* sees patterns hidden from the rest of us mere mortals; Daniel *sometimes* sees angels and the like. And me, as I said before, I *occasionally* heal people. I have no control over the when, the why, or the where. It's a great gift when it works, but since I don't know when it works it confuses me and that makes me shy away from trying.

Am I afraid to fail? No. Yes. I don't know. Perhaps this doesn't make sense. When I was still in college, I had to take a class in basic psychology. Almost everyone did. The professor told us about a study where two monkeys were given a shock, every now and again. They shocked one monkey on a regular schedule. Same time of day, and same number of times. That monkey didn't like it, but learned to live with it. The other monkey was shocked at random. That poor thing went nuts.

I don't admit this often, but more and more I feel like the second monkey.

Sleep finally came, but it was loaded with extra-real dreams, not one of which I liked. I didn't sleep long, maybe a few hours. I didn't know. I didn't care. The bed was done with me and I was done with it.

I swung my feet over the side of the bed, then stopped short. The pain in my back had grown sharper, and a new set of pains had set in to my knees and one of my feet—the foot I injured playing football. It hurt more now than it did then, and trust me, it hurt a lot back then.

It took two tries for me to hoist my bulk off the mattress. I took a few steps and each one hurt, but as I moved along the joints loosened up some. My first thought was to blame the mattress. That changed when I hobbled into the bathroom and turned on the light. The image in the mirror made me forget why I had gone into the bathroom in the first place. The man in the mirror was me all right, but I had changed. Not greatly, but I've been looking at my mug for over two decades and I could tell that my skin seemed a tad more loose, and my hair a bit thinner. I leaned closer to the mirror. There were wrinkles around the eyes and my hair was longer.

I had aged. I didn't need to think that through. Helsa had told us we would, but I didn't expect it to happen during a short nap. I could tell this was an uneven process. I had grown some beard stubble, but not enough to match the age of my face. Why that should be, I have no idea, and I doubted I could figure it out.

I like to put things in the best possible light so I told myself how glad I was that I hadn't slept longer. I also realized whatever it was we were supposed to do, we needed to get to it. Tick-tock, tock-tick, the clock. I now understood what the Tockity man meant. And I didn't like it.

No more wasting time. I doubted I had any time to waste. I dressed again and left my room. I knew my destination and I was there in short order, maybe a little slower than I would have made the trip when I first got to this place, but I didn't let any moss grow on me.

I didn't use the communication panel on the side of the doorway to the hospital ward. I just walked in. Nurses looked at me but said nothing. I had a feeling they were thinking, "He'll be in here permanently soon enough."

No lingering for me. I came to work; to lay it all on the line. If I failed, it would be a failure of trying to do something right.

No need to tell the nurses what I intended to do. They wouldn't understand me anyway. I stopped at the nearest bed. A man who looked to be well north of ninety met my gaze. I doubt he saw me. Cataracts covered his eyes. I took one of his hands in my mine and laid my other hand on his forehead.

I prayed.

I prayed for all I was worth. Some minutes passed before I could open my eyes. No change. The cataracts were still there, and the old man/kid was still the same as I first saw him. No healing.

I moved to the next bed, then the next. Same result, by which I mean no results. Maybe my gift didn't work in this universe. Maybe I forgot how to do it right. Maybe I had fallen out of favor with God. My eyes grew wet again. Still, I moved from one patient to the next doing absolutely no good at all. The children were all dying of old age.

Time walked by, tock-tick, tockity, tockity, tick, tick, tick. With each tick I felt more despair and more anger. I didn't think I could slip lower. Turns out, I could.

The door to the room opened and a familiar looking young man walked in. He wore a robe and was barefoot. His hair hung to his ears and was styled in the I-just-rolled-outta-bed look. I wondered if he was a new patient, then the ceiling collapsed on me. Daniel.

The young man stepped to the bedside of the eight-year-old kid who looked eighty. He took her hand and just stood there. A weak giggle rose from the bed and I stood glued to the floor as Daniel stroked the patient's hair.

If I had died at that moment, I would have considered it a blessing worthy of the highest praise. One of the nurses wheeled a chair over to Daniel so he could sit vigil. He took it. Sat. Then began to weep as the heart monitor next the bed flat-lined.

I limped to his side put a hand first on his shoulder then on the dead woman's arm. I needed to speak, but I had no words; I needed to grant comfort but had none to give. I was useless.

Daniel laid his head on the side of the bed, resting it on their clasped hands.

My weeping joined Daniel's.

BRENDA AND ANDI walked through the doors. Apparently they didn't bother to check-in, either. They took three steps in, then saw us. Daniel hadn't moved; his head still rested on the bed. The dead girl/woman had been staring at the ceiling. I closed her eyes. I wish I could have done more. All I could do was stand near Daniel until the nurses thought enough time had passed and came to take her away.

Brenda stopped in her tracks. She was holding Daniel's clothes; clothes that fit an eight-year-old.

The young man in the robe must have looked familiar to her but it was still impossible to believe. I believed it. I could see gray in Brenda's hair and wrinkles in Andi's face. They weren't old, but they had definitely aged.

Brenda's eyes shifted from Daniel to the person in the bed, to the heart monitor, to me, then back to Daniel. "Oh, baby boy," she said. She stepped beside Daniel, bent and hugged him. That's when the sniffing started. Andi came to my side, took a look at me, then let the tears flow.

"I couldn't do anything." I whispered the words, at the moment it was the only volume setting I had. "I tried, Andi, I really tried. I prayed for each one. I tried to heal them, but it didn't work. I feel useless."

She took my arm, leaned in and rested her head on my shoulder. Any other time, any other place, any other universe, I would have been over the moon. I was none of that. I was just heartbroken.

Minutes tock-ticked by, then an idea occurred to me. "We have to get these people back."

"How?" Andi kept squeezing my arm like she feared her legs would give way.

"I don't know. I just know we have to do it. I can't let these kids die one by one, and I can't let . . . others . . . be brought over—"

"Tank?" Andi let go and turned to face me. "What are you thinking?"

"I'm not sure yet . . ." A fresh thought arrived. It was like someone was dictating directions to me. "Andi, I need your help. You too, Brenda."

Daniel finally raised his head. "What about me?" He wiped his eyes dry.

"I always need you, buddy." I started to call him "little buddy," but that didn't seem to fit anymore.

"We have to get Daniel back home." Brenda sounded desperate. That made sense. We were all facing the same death. "Littlefoot returned to her proper age when she got back to her world; maybe we'll do the same when we get back to ours."

"I was thinking the same thing." My mind was hitting on all cylinders. "Andi, talk to the other patients. Ask questions. Find a pattern. We need a pattern."

"Daniel needs some clothes to wear."

"I bet Helsa can get him something." A motion to my right drew my attention to a nurse on a phone. A few moments later, Helsa walked in.

Chapter 12

DOING SOMETHING EVEN IF IT'S WRONG

MY MOTHER USED to say that a watched pot never boils. Of course, she meant the water in the pot, but I never corrected her. She used to say that a lot. In our family, she was the one that had all the patience. I'm pretty good at patience, but not great. Especially if lives were at stake, I get positively antsy.

Andi was my watched pot. Helsa, Brenda, Daniel—Helsa brought a police uniform for Daniel to wear and a pair of shoes—and I went to the cafeteria, not to eat, but to meet. It was easier to talk around a cafeteria table. More elbow room.

We did very little talking. I didn't know where to start. "Hey Daniel, what's it feel like to go from kid to teenager overnight? Are you diggin' that?" That would be as stupid as it sounds. So instead, we played with our drinks and I tried to get my brain to be better than it was. It was wearing me out. I had only been up a few hours and I was already wishing for a nap. Growing older ain't for sissies.

Brenda broke the silence. "You gotta plan, Cowboy?"

"Not really. Just a few thousand questions."

"Me neither."

"We have to save the kids." Daniel's voice was nearly an octave deeper. It was interesting to hear, but I wanted my little buddy to be, well, little again.

"I know." I rubbed my eyes. My vision wasn't as sharp as I was used too. No doubt I needed glasses. "I'll do anything I can." I'm pretty secure about myself. I know I'm not the brain in our group. I'm fine with that. I'm just a big lug God has seen fit to use. At least, that's how I saw it.

"We got here," Daniel said. "We can get back."

He lifted his eyes and looked around. From time to time Daniel sees angels and I've been with the kid long enough to know he was looking for his friends. His expression told me he was disappointed.

THROUGH THE OPEN door to the cafeteria I saw Andi and Helsa approaching. I was just getting used to seeing Helsa as an adult; it would take longer for me to get used to seeing an older Andi. Still, she looked good.

Andi walked with her head down as if following a line on the floor. Others might look at her and think, "Uh-oh, she has bad news." They'd be wrong. Andi's brain worked in a different way than the rest of us. Her brain was burning rubber and I took that to mean something good.

Andi sat across the table and next to Brenda; Helsa sat next to me.

We waited for Andi to speak. I knew she would when she got her thoughts in order. I didn't have to wait long.

Andi said, "Okay, I'm gonna spew."

"Eww," Daniel said.

"I don't mean that. I'm gonna spew what I've learned and then we can try to sort it out. Okay?"

No one objected.

"I've talked to as many of the patients as could speak. A few were showing signs of senility but even then, I got a few things. Tank, you were right, they are children. The youngest is six and the oldest is twelve. There is no pattern to their ages. It's a mix of those ages and all of the ones in between. There is roughly an even ratio of males to females but there are a few more girls than guys. Again, no real pattern there. It's what we'd expect if we visited any hospital: girls outnumber boys by a slight margin. So whoever or whatever is doing this is no respecter of persons or genders."

"Is it only children who are dragged into this world?" I felt silly the moment I asked it.

"Think about it, Tank. You, Brenda and I are adults and we came over just like Daniel.

"The adults have died off already," I said. Those words tasted bitter.

"Right. We established that yesterday."

I remembered. I just wanted her to know I was listening. Either that or my memory was getting a little wobbly.

Andi went on, her eyes looking around the table but never really seeing us. She was immersed in thought. "All of them are from Newland. That realization is important. If we had people here from different towns, states, even other parallel universes, it would mean the problem is too large for us to handle. Of course, it might still be too much for us, but at least we're dealing with just one place that is somehow tied to this reality."

She paused. "Remember the mousey hotel manager we met when we came into town?"

"I do," Brenda said. "She needed a good backhand to the face, if you ask me."

"Because . . ." Andi prompted.

"Because she tried to run us off, that's why." Brenda said. "You were there. If she could have shoved us out the door, she would have done it."

"And Tiffany at the café?" Andi said.

"Same thing. She tried to get us to head out of town."

"They don't like strangers," I said.

"Sorry, Tank. You're wrong. So are you, Brenda. And as much as I hate to admit it, so was I. They weren't trying to get us to move on because they didn't like tourists, they were trying to save us—to keep us from becoming the next set of victims."

That was a punch to the gut. Like Brenda, I assumed they just didn't like our looks.

"They could have been clearer about that." Brenda was not ready to give up a perfectly good bad mood.

"Not really, Brenda. They couldn't say, 'Enjoy your stay in Newland, North Carolina, oh, and don't let anyone make you disappear.'" Andi took a deep breath, as if revealing this information was wearing her out. "They have lost family members and sometimes their children without the slightest hint of what happened to them. We have the advantage of knowing a little about where we are."

"I misjudged them," I said.

Andi agreed. "We all did."

Helsa said, "When all this began a few months ago, I did some checking. To our knowledge, people from your world only show up in New Land and no place else in our world."

Her eyes turned yellow. That was a new one.

"Not many days ago," Andi said, "we sat in a university auditorium to listen to the professor talk about alternate dimensions and parallel universes. As you know, I made the PowerPoint slides and helped organize his material, just like I've done for the professor over the last few years. He initially planned to include some controversial material, but took it out about a week before we went to Tampa. He couldn't provide enough evidence that the events he planned to describe were in fact real and not pure fiction. I helped with that research. Very interesting, but not substantial."

"Like what?" I asked.

"Okay, just understand that some of this may be real and some of it might be pure baloney."

Andi took a deep breath as if she were planning on spewing information again. Which she was.

"There have been reports of people, groups, and even civilizations that have vanished. In 1872, the steamboat *Iron Mountain* disappeared while making its way in the Mississippi. She was never heard from again. Unfortunately, only one newspaper reported the vanishing. So did it really happen? Who knows?

"In 1947 a small plane crashed on Mt. Rainier. When searchers found the crash site they discovered evidence of injury, but no people, no bodies, no footprints, and no indication that predators had hauled bodies away. The pilot and passengers were just gone."

Andi fiddled with Brenda's napkin. We gave her a moment to collect her thoughts. "In the late 1800s, on a farm outside Gallatin, Tennessee, a farmer named David Lang went into his field one day and—in full view of his family—disappeared. Some say the family could hear his voice in the field calling for help, but they could never find him. That mystery was never solved.

"It's a long list," Andi continued. "The Eskimo village of Anjikuni was found empty of all its residents, but everything they owned was left behind. A large group of Spanish soldiers vanished in 1711. Don't even get me started on the Bermuda Triangle."

"Are you saying that all these things really happened?" Brenda asked.

"No, I'm not. But we've seen enough in our adventures to make me wonder. The professor, of course, dismissed these stories, but I had a feeling he wondered if he might be wrong about that. But you know him—he was the poster child for logic and the scientific method."

This kind of talk tends to fry my brain, but I had a sense that Andi had more connections to make.

"Man, I could use a cup of coffee," Andi said. She looked worn out.

I started to rise, but Helsa beat me to it. She returned with more coffee for every one, including Daniel. I still didn't know if it was really coffee, but it looked and smelled close enough.

A couple of sips later, Andi continued. "I tried to nail down exact times when the kids were brought over or sent over or whatever the right verb is, but we're dealing with children and they don't fixate on time like adults do. If some of the adults were still alive, I might have made more progress. Anyway, I learned that there is no clear pattern. It's not like they arrive on a timetable. Helsa confirmed that for me. They keep records of arrival times here. The time between arrivals vary and I can't figure out a pattern on that. For all I know, new folk may show up before lunch or not for a week. I doubt time here is exactly the same as home." She turned to Helsa. "How long does it take for your world to circle the sun?"

"Three hundred and seventy days, of course."

Andi did blink at that. "How long is a day?"

"Twenty-six hours."

Andi turned to the rest of us. "The year here is five days longer, and each day is roughly two hours longer." She rubbed her face. "I imagine a minute here is different than a minute back home. It would take me some time to figure all that out, and there's a good chance I'd fail even if I tried."

"So we got nothin'," Brenda said.

"Very little, I agree, but I did notice that the transition place, if that's a good term for it, was not always the same. We were in Tiffany's Café when we were snatched; others were in front of the café, at the end of town, in their homes, or some other place." Andi slouched in her seat as if telling us all this had drained her. Maybe it did, but I'm pretty sure she was feeling like a failure.

Andi sighed in a way that broke my heart.

"You did good, Andi."

"Thanks, Tank, but I've come up short— "

"Paper." It was Daniel.

I looked at him. He held the watch he had taken from the professor's room as a keepsake. Initially the watch proved too big for the arm of a ten-year-old. Since Daniel's unwelcome growth spirt, the watch almost fit. Not quite, but almost.

"What?" I said.

"Paper. Please." Daniel didn't look at me. Instead, he gazed at Helsa.

She nodded, rose, and left the cafeteria only to return a few moments later with a couple of pads of paper. She also carried a pen and a pencil, covering the bases, I supposed, and set them in front of Daniel.

"Whatcha going to do with that, baby?" Brenda said.

His answer was an action: he pushed the material in front of Brenda. "Draw. The town. Draw the town."

"I'm sorry, Daniel, but I didn't pay much attention to the place."

"Tank did. He took a walk."

Brenda looked at me, then at Andi. "I don't get it."

"Draw." Daniel was insistent. Usually he kept to himself, living much of his life in his own mind, but he had no problem jumping into the middle of things if he had something to contribute.

Brenda took the pencil and started by drawing the main street we used to get into town. I outlined my walk, mentioning buildings I had seen and houses I had passed. Brenda added those to the map. Twenty minutes later we had a pretty decent map of Newland.

The moment Brenda set the pencil down, Daniel grabbed the paper pad and pushed it in front of Andi. She blinked a few times, looked at me, met Brenda's eyes, then let her gaze settle on Daniel.

"I think I get it," she said. With that, Andi picked up the pencil.

THE WISDOM OF DANIEL

I WAS PACING, my patience gone. I had a feeling that we were about to cross a threshold of understanding and wanted to pray that we would recognize it. I pray on my feet, a lot. Pacing helps me focus. I'm sure some psychologist somewhere could tell me the why and wherefore of that, but I wasn't interested in knowing then and I'm no more interested in knowing now.

Andi was putting little circles on the map Brenda had drawn. Each circle represented some child from our world who who was dying in this world. Next to each circle Andi wrote two numbers in tiny script.

"This number is the subject's age; this one the day when the transfer occurred." There were many circles with only numbers, the patients didn't know or couldn't remember the day and time their problems began.

I assumed that the circles would be all over the proverbial map but even I could see a trend. The markers formed a line from Tiffany's Café to the old church. Another line was formed going north from the church and into the residential area I had walked a couple of days ago. Granted, these lines were a bit squiggly, but it was a pattern.

"There may be a time pattern after all." Andi didn't look up from the hand-drawn map. "I've included our event in Tiffany's. It's the most recent event we know of." She let her gaze linger on the paper. I leaned over the table for a closer look. "Odd."

"What's odd?" I leaned even closer to the page.

"I was expecting a straight line, or a clump of events, but I don't see that at all." Andi pointed at the old church with the pretty steeple. "If I . . . Can it be that simple?"

"I don't see it, so it's not all that simple to me," I said.

"It looks like all the events fan out from the church building, like spokes from a hub." The earliest events happened in the residential area, the most recent in the heart of town."

"And what does that mean?" Helsa asked.

"Notice how the clumps of circles—people—are associated on one line, then the next taken are a little distance from the first. The same can be said for the other small groups." She scratched her head. "Think of the church as a lighthouse with a beam of light that swings in a big circle. Maybe I can extrapolate the next line—the line along which another abduction might occur."

She didn't have a ruler, so Andi tore a strip of paper from the edge of the page and used it to mark the distance between "spokes" at the same point from the hub, the church.

"The bar," Andi said. "My best guess is that the next group will come from the bar."

"At least there won't be any children in a bar." That was some comfort to me but it wasn't enough. "This is useful information, but I don't know what to do with it." I began pacing again. "If you're right about the place, Andi, we still don't have clue about the time."

Andi nodded slowly. "True. I don't know how to figure that out. The time of the previous events seem random."

"I suppose we could move into the place and—"

"Guys?"

It was Brenda. I had been so absorbed in what Andi was doing that I had forgotten her. One look told me she hadn't been sitting on her hands. She had made use of the pen Helsa had brought after Andi glommed onto the pencil. While we had been talking, Brenda was having a go at one of the other pads of paper. This could be good, or it could be bad. Brenda pushed the paper to the middle of the table. She pointed a finger at the middle of the page.

She had drawn the front of the bar we had driven past when we came to town and I had walked past on my little hike. "Him. He's the key. Get him and we get our answers."

In front of the bar stood Tockity Man and in front of Tockity Man was another figure. A big figure holding the one-eyed man with the cardboard eye patch by the throat and with his other hand he was holding Tockity's fist. The big man was me.

There was something else in the drawing: a large vehicle.

"What is that?" I tapped the image. Brenda didn't draw the whole vehicle, just something that looked like the back end of a bus."

"Beats me," Brenda said. "I just draw this stuff."

Helsa took a gander, furrowed her brow a little, squinted, then suddenly straightened. "It's a bus."

I felt good about my guess, but why would Brenda draw the tail end of a bus.

Helsa blinked a few times. "It's a school bus." Her eyes widened. "That's it."

"What's it?" I asked.

Andi was already dialed in. "It's our clock, Tank. It's our clock. School buses run on a schedule."

"It's headed away from the school," Helsa said. "So that means school is out. I'll be right back."

Helsa moved to a phone mounted to the wall about ten feet from us. No one had to tell me what she was doing. She was calling the school.

The thing about Brenda and her drawings is this—she is never wrong.

Chapter 14

A STEP OF FAITH

I HAD NO idea if any of this would work. It was one of those things that looked good on paper, but seemed beyond stupid when said out loud. I was desperate to do something. Too many lives had already been lost, and children who barely knew how to live were facing the death that should be limited to the old. I was older. Okay, fine. Andi and Brenda had aged, but they had already lived a good bit of life. Yet the kids in the ward knew nothing of first love, hopes, or dreams. Some were just old enough to learn to throw a ball. I had to do something and I trusted Brenda's and Andi's insights.

The van we were riding in moved down the hill, driven by one of the policemen we had met when we first arrived in New Land. When we first met, he was all smiles. Now he was as sober as an undertaker. Once I told Helsa what I wanted to do, she sprang into action. Clearly, she carried some kind of weight in this strange building. When she spoke, people hopped to it.

Helsa sat next to me in one of the van's rear seats. I leaned toward her. "I haven't asked this before, Littlefoot, because it reminds me of when you left us. Watching you go was as much pain as I've ever felt."

She took my hand. "I still love that name. Littlefoot. I cherish it."

That gave me a grin. "How did you get back here?"

"They brought me back. The people who send you places sent me there; they brought me home."

"How?"

She shook her head. "I don't know. It's beyond me. They know more than we do. They do good for the world, several worlds."

"Do you know who they are?"

She looked sad. "No, Tank, I don't. I really don't. So much mystery. So many unknowns."

"We feel the same. Still, we've done some good things. How did they send you to our world and bring you back?"

"They set up a machine. I don't think it created an opening between our worlds, but, he said it kept the doorway open."

"*He?*"

She looked away, then said a name that sounded like Shaun or maybe Shane. I don't think it was Shaun, but it was close.

"Where is he now?"

"I don't know. After I got back, he disappeared. It took me a little time to return to my proper age. When I did, he was missing."

"He was part of your team?"

She nodded. "In a way, he was much like your professor. I'm a bit like Andi. When I was my natural age again—that took about three weeks—my team was off doing the work we do. They never came back."

"No idea what happened to them?"

"None, but . . . I can't be sure, but I have a bad feeling about Shaun. I think he might be your Tockity Man."

That was a shocker. "What makes you think that?" I tried to keep all the surprise out of my voice. I doubt that I succeeded.

Tears filled her eyes. "He was the one that operated the device that kept the doorway to your world open long enough for me to pass through. After my team went missing, I went to the building were we kept the device. It's at the end of town. The device was gone."

"The church?" I asked.

"It is a center for worship. Yes. *Was* a center for worship. The spiritual ways are not followed here as they once were."

"Same can be said for our world," I said.

"It would explain a few things if this guy made off with the equipment and brought it to our world."

"Again, I can't say that's what happened, but I fear it might be as you say."

"Why would he do that?" Brenda asked.

Helsa gazed out the window for a moment. "If it is Shaun, then I think he lost his mind. It's one of the dangers of jumping between universes. It short-circuits our brains."

"Tockity Man is more than a little crazy." That may have been harsh. I patted Helsa's hand. "This isn't easy work. We can only do what we can do."

Helsa's revelation was painful to hear and I'm sure even more painful to share. I wondered what it was like wondering what happened to a team you had spent so much time with. The thought of losing Andi and Brenda would feel like someone doing surgery on me with a butter knife.

WE ARRIVED IN front of the building that corresponded to the bar in our Newland, except here, best I could tell, it was more of a juice bar.

Helsa spoke to her driver, who repeated the words over the radio. The patrol cars that had followed us back into town blocked off the road. Other patrol cars, probably teams already on duty, were stationed along the street. Officers slipped from the vehicles and moved to the bar, walked through the door. Moments later patrons exited, looking confused. So did one man who I took to be the owner. He was less than happy.

"You ready to rock-and-roll, Cowboy?" Brenda sounded confident. I'm pretty sure she was faking it.

"No, but let's do this anyway."

The moment we were outside the van, I heard Helsa: "Tank."

She rushed me and threw her arms around my neck, kissed me on both cheeks, then stepped back. "If it is Shaun and if he has the transport mechanism, then he'll have an activator. It looks like a small red fruit. Don't let him use it, or everything will be for nothing."

I carried a long coil of rope into the business. I had been right. It was a juice bar.

Dropping the coil of rope on the floor, I pulled one end up and tied it around my waist. A uniformed officer tied the other end to a stool bolted to the floor. We had a plan. It didn't make a lot of sense, but it was the only plan we could come up with. We had a likely location for the next set of abductees. Andi figured that out. Brenda's future-drawing power had taken the next step giving us a pretty good time and placing me at the scene with Tockity. Since Brenda's drawing showed me mixing it up with the one-eyed crazy man in this universe, it meant I somehow needed to bring him here. All we had to do was get to the bar before the event.

"I hope this works," I said. "If it doesn't, then you guys will never let me forget it."

"You got that right, Cowboy." I turned to see Brenda grinning. That did me a lot of good. She could fill a room with laughter or suck all the air out of it with just a few words. Love that girl.

When we were dragged from our world we were sitting in a café booth. I didn't see anything like a portal or door, but then again I was looking at my breakfast. I hoped I would recognize it when it arrived. I scanned the interior of the juice bar with its blenders, brightly upholstered seats, and artwork of some strange looking fruit on the walls. We moved the small tables and chairs from the middle of the floor. I figured if I stood in the centered of the room I would have the shortest possible distance to anything that appeared in the room.

A light flashed in my eyes, the same kind of light that flashed in my head when we were transported here. Problem. The light didn't form a structure like a door or anything. It was just a glow that filled almost half of the space in the juice bar. I hesitated, wondering where to enter.

Then I got a break: two or three confused and shaken people emerged from the center of the glow. I didn't hesitate. I charge the point where I had seen them materialize. I might have only a moment. I hoped that I wouldn't run through it and slam into the wall.

I didn't.

The light that surrounded me now filled me. And it hurt. Big time pain. I may have screamed. If I did, I didn't hear it.

Then the light was gone and I was doubled over but standing on a floor covered in peanut shells.

The bar.

"Tockity, tockity, tick—"

I straightened, and saw the scruffy man with the Corn Flakes eye patch. A moment later, I had him by the throat. He had something in his right hand. It looked like the device Helsa described. With my freehand I clamped my big mitt around his hand and squeezed until I was sure I had control of all his fingers. His face twisted in pain and it told me I had accomplished that part of my goal.

"Is your name Shaun?"

He looked surprised, then confused, then I drove my forehead into his face. He stopped struggling.

I released his throat, and took hold of the front of his filthy coat. The rope around my waist served as my guide back to portal. All I had to do was make sure that Tockity didn't regain consciousness and wiggle his hand with the activator free. If he did, and he might close the gateway with me on this side, and my friends on the other; my friends and all those old kids who needed help. I dragged him along as if he were a doll. I'll admit it. I was a little pumped up on adrenaline and fear. A few steps later we were back in the other universe.

I DRAGGED THE unconscious Tockity Man to the side of the juice bar, ordering some patrons who had been snatched from the liquor bar out of the way. It was natural that they would be confused, but the liquor wasn't doing them any favors.

"Back. Go back." Helsa was loud and forceful. Still they—six men and two women—wasn't sure it was a wise idea. Helsa stepped to the spot where I had crossed over and pointed. "Go! Run!"

They stood still, confused into inaction.

"NOW!" That was Brenda. She was more convincing. They followed the police officer's directions if for no other reason than to save their hearing from another Brenda outburst.

I pinned Tockity to the wall. He was still out of it, but he could come to anytime and I was afraid of letting go of his hand. I wanted the threshold open as long as possible.

Helsa was overseeing the rest of the plan. Officers and nurses poured through the door of the juice bar helping elderly patients into the light. Some were on gurneys, some hobbled, some were carried by police officers. None of the helpers questioned Helsa when she told them to carry their patients into the light, turn around and come right back.

"Brenda, Daniel, go through. Take charge over there." They exchanged glances and marched through. "You too, Andi."

"I'm not leaving you, Tank."

"Andi, please, just go. I'll be there as soon as I can. Go, those kids need help. Go."

She went.

Moments later helpers were returning, shaken, pale, and few vomiting, but they kept at it. Time and time again, they carried patients into the white void until every elderly child had crossed over. Helsa spit out orders like a drill sergeant. Based on the way I felt, I guessed those brave souls might need a few days off.

Tockity came to in a fury. His fingernails dug into my face. His knee caught me in the groin. I was already half out of things from traveling through the opening twice in short order. I didn't need such treatment.

Some of the officers came to my aide. We took him to the floor, pinned his right arm and slowly pried his fingers back until I held what looked like a small, glowing red apple. It had a switch on it. Tockity had it pressed when I grabbed his hand so I kept it pressed.

"Easy with that, Tank. It's your only way home."

I released Tockity to the cops. Stood. Wobbled a little and did my best to keep the contents of my stomach right where they were.

"Go, Tank," Helsa said.

"I need a minute with you."

"No. The activator could stop working. It's not in the same universe as the device it controls. Go. Go now."

107

I had already watched Helsa—Littlefoot—fade in front of my eyes, so I didn't want to say good-bye again.

"Helsa—"

"Shut up. I can't go with you and you can't stay here. If either one of us tries, then we die. Go. Your friends need you."

I walked to the light and looked back.

"Keep up the good work, Tank," she said. "You're a hero. You're my hero."

My vision blurred. My face was hot.

I walked through the light.

I was weeping when I emerged back in my own world. I don't care who knows it.

Epilogue

IT TOOK SEVERAL tries, but we were able to take the door to the church down. The sledgehammers we carried made it easy. With me were several men from Newland, each had a sledgehammer that he either brought from home or had been given by the owner of the hardware store. He was with us, too. After all, he had lost his wife, but got his eight-year-old daughter back. There were ten of us, all total, and each had a similar story.

I felt a little bad about breaking into a church, even one that had been abandoned a long time ago. Still, a church is a group of believers, not a building, so I put my reservations aside and helped knock the door in.

We found the device that bridged the two universes. The sanctuary had no pews. It was a wide open space with the device. It was an odd looking duck. It reminded me of some bit of abstract sculpture. I don't know what I expected. Maybe something sleek and shiny. It wasn't sleek. It looked like a golf ball but instead of all those little indentations it was covered in little metal bumps. It wasn't shiny either. I could tell it was metal but it lacked the luster of aluminum. It looked a tad corroded. I doubt Tockity took care of his toys.

It rested on a set of wood blocks. High tech meets low tech. An electrical line ran from the bottom of the sphere and had been wired into a junction box in one of the walls.

I wondered how it worked but only for a few moments. I had other plans for the thing.

It was a little difficult to explain all that happened to the others, but since we had brought many of their children back they would have believed us if we had said the moon was made of chocolate.

We waited as Walter, the local electrician, disengaged the power to the unit, then I removed a small paper sack from my pocket, opened it, and removed a slip of paper with a name on it. It was no secret that we had come to destroy the thing but it needed to be done with some dignity, not like a crazed mob. These people needed to a have a hand in ending the problem. This was the best idea I could come up with. Tiffany knew everyone who had lost loved ones. She put us in contact with them. When I told them what I had in mind, not a man said no.

I want to make sure everyone got a good whack at the thing. So, I wrote their names on slips of paper, got a brown paper lunch bag, dumped them in and created my own little lottery.

"Gerald Ames."

Gerald grinned, but he did so with tears in his eyes. He got his son back, but was shaken to the core to see what had happened to the boy. They were all shaken. It took awhile, but we convinced them that the impossible would happen and their children would grow young again. Those who didn't get their kids back, well, we couldn't do anything but weep with them. And we did a lot of that.

The group of men stepped away to give Gerald a little room and Gerald gave it all he had. He was in his forties, but looked to me like he was well acquainted with hard work. The business end of the sledge struck a devastating first blow.

A cheer went up.

Gerald folded over in tears and regret. Several men went to his side while I pulled another name from the bag. "Jensen P. Monroe. You ready, brother?"

"More ready than I can say." He recited the name of his two children who had been returned to him, then the names of his neighbor's children who were forever gone, then he put every fiber of this body into his swing. The sound of it hurt my ears.

"Luke Morris . . ."

THE CHILDREN WERE housed in the hotel at the end of the street. Two entire floors had been converted to a hospital wing. The local doctor, a young man not long out of med school, and a few nurses he called in to help, tended to the children.

Andi brought them up to date. "You're not going to believe this," she began, but the doctor lived in the town and knew the score. The two nurses soon learned that all that Andi had told them was right. I can't say enough good about them.

We stayed a week. Daniel began to look a couple of years younger and was having trouble finding the right size clothing. I guess it's true, you can't keep kids in clothes no matter if they're growing up or down.

As for the adults, we were returning to our proper ages, more slowly than I liked, but I could be patient. At least I was in the right universe.

Each night I spent a little time looking at the stars and wondering about Littlefoot. I guess I will always do that.

ONCE THE CAR was packed we said our goodbyes to Jewel, the hotel owner, and thanked her for making her place available for the kids to recuperate in. We also thanked her for trying to save our necks by sending us packing.

Before we entered the car, Brenda called us close. "We saved a lot of children," she said. "That makes me feel pretty good. And Daniel was a big part of that. We might not have learned what we needed to know if he didn't insist on some paper and started bossing us around."

We all agreed to that. I figured there was more coming out.

"Daniel and me had a chat. Okay, he did the chatting and I did the listening. You know him, he's not much on conversation, but he did make it clear that he was part of the team and even though he's only ten, he's a very different ten than other boys."

"That's a fact," I said.

Brenda looked at the ground. "Anyway, forget all that Batman stuff I was throwin' around." Except she didn't use the word "stuff."

"Oh, man, and here I was thinking we finally got rid of you."

She punched me in the arm. It hurt in a wonderful way. "I will take you down, Cowboy. You know I will."

"Yes, ma'am, I do know that."

Then I hugged her. That led to a group hug.

And a prayer of thanksgiving from me.

ABOUT ALTON L. GANSKY

Alton L. Gansky (Al) is the author of 24 novels and
nine nonfiction works, as well as principal writer of
nine novels and two nonfiction books. He has been
a Christy Award finalist (*A Ship Possessed*) and an
Angel Award winner (*Terminal Justice*) and recently
received the ACFW award for best suspense/
thriller for his work on *Fallen Angel*. He holds a BA
and MA in biblical studies and was granted a Litt.D.
He lives in central California with his wife.

www.altongansky.com

Don't miss *Piercing the Veil*, the next installment of the Harbingers Series!

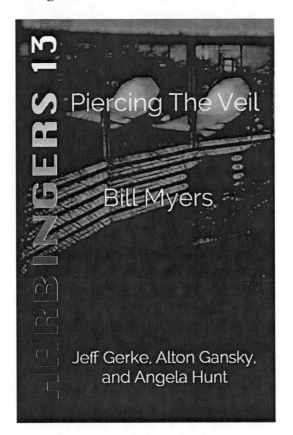

CPSIA information can be obtained at www.ICGtesting.com
Printed in the USA
LVOW10s2158240816

501735LV00014B/282/P